"I'm ready. This is ready."

He indicated the beautiful resort with a thrust of his head.

"But I'm not ready for what comes later. The leaving part. And I'm not sure what to do about that, Josie."

"Resign yourself, because time has a way of marching on." She kept it light on purpose, he was sure, but not before he spotted that now-familiar flash of regret. She moved back slightly.

"You're right. And for now I've got to get Addie home to bed. Tomorrow's going to come early. Mom and Dad are taking over with Addie for the next two weeks while we get things ironed out here. And then—"

"Another chapter unfolds." Josie leaned down and waved to Addie in the back seat. "See you later, sweet thing! Thanks for letting me tag along today!"

"Bye, Josie!"

She didn't turn back his way. She didn't pause to flirt. True to her word, Josie kept a distance he wished he could broach, but unless he was willing to take a whole new turn in life, she was right to walk away.

Multipublished bestselling author **Ruth Logan Herne** loves God, her country, her family, dogs, chocolate and coffee! Married to a very patient man, she lives in an old farmhouse in upstate New York and thinks possums should leave the cat food alone and snakes should always live outside. There are no exceptions to either rule! Visit Ruth at ruthloganherne.com.

Books by Ruth Logan Herne

Love Inspired

Grace Haven

An Unexpected Groom
Her Unexpected Family
Their Surprise Daddy
The Lawman's Yuletide Baby
Her Secret Daughter

Kirkwood Lake

The Lawman's Second Chance
Falling for the Lawman
The Lawman's Holiday Wish
Loving the Lawman
Her Holiday Family

Men of Allegany County

Mended Hearts
Yuletide Hearts
His Mistletoe Family

Visit the Author Profile page at Harlequin.com for more titles.

Her Secret Daughter

Ruth Logan Herne

HARLEQUIN® LOVE INSPIRED®

Recycling programs
for this product may
not exist in your area.

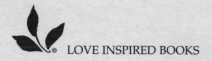

LOVE INSPIRED BOOKS

ISBN-13: 978-1-335-42789-2

Her Secret Daughter

www.Harlequin.com

Printed in U.S.A.

For I know him, that he will command his children and his household after him, and they shall keep the way of the Lord, to do justice and judgment; that the Lord may bring upon Abraham that which he hath spoken of him.

—*Genesis* 18:19

Jon Jamison…this one's for you. A book about a wonderful father who truly loves his children and doesn't scold too much when their grandmother gives them copious amounts of chocolate milk and treats. I love you, Jon!

Chapter One

Josie Gallagher gripped the letter from the county manager's office with tight hands.

She already knew the contents. Cruz Maldonado, her cousin Rory's husband and a lawyer, had called with a heads-up the night before. She'd lost her battle against the hotel giant erecting a five-star resort just south of her popular lakeside barbecue joint. Her little place stood in the way of progress, which meant she'd have to relocate the Bayou Barbecue. She tore open the envelope, and her gaze landed on four distinct words. "Eminent domain petition granted."

Gone.

Just like that. Her hard work, dedication and years of working with some of the best chefs in New Orleans had dissipated like a whiff of hickory smoke because the boat-launch site on her land was a better match for the major hotelier. Her lake access was about to become the property of Carrington Hotels & Inns for a tidy sum to help her launch a new spot, but new spots weren't exactly a given along the waterfront, and real estate had gone sky-high in Grace Haven, New York.

"Bad news?" Her cousin Kimberly came in through the side door of Josie's tiny apartment. The three-room living quarters was attached to the Southern-style eatery she'd spent years building, which meant she wasn't only out of a job. She was also out of a home. "Is that from the county?"

Josie fought back a wealth of angry words she'd like to say. Clutching the stupid paper, she nodded. "Yup."

"Oh, Josie." Kimberly hugged her, and it felt good to be hugged. "I'm so sorry. Are you sure we can't continue to fight? Take it further?"

They'd already gone the legal route Cruz had recommended, but he'd been honest from the beginning. If the county saw a need for this strip of land to provide the proper spacing for a major player, it'd have Carrington pay fair market value and take the land. End of story. "It's done."

"How long have you got to vacate?"

"Thirty days."

"Thirty days?" Anger darkened Kimberly's gaze. She was nearly nine months pregnant with her second child, and Josie didn't want to tip her into labor, but at least a new baby would be a happy end to an otherwise wretched day. "They can't possibly expect you to take care of moving everything from your home and business and find a new place in thirty days. Can they? That's preposterous, Josie, even for Southerners."

A deep and distinctly Southern drawl interrupted them from the screened door. "It would seem less preposterous had you taken the initial offer six months ago."

The women turned. A man stood at the door, midthirties. Crazy good-looking. He had an official-looking folder in his left hand, which meant he was most likely another Carrington Hotels henchman. Kimberly must have sensed the same thing because she folded her arms above the baby bump in total defensive Gallagher posture.

Josie Gallagher moved forward, determined to save Kimberly from herself. "This is a private meeting, and I'm pretty sure you weren't invited, sir."

The man pointed south. "Carrington Hotels has been nothing but courteous about this whole thing. We approached you personally, and you laughed at our representative, and from what I've heard, possibly also shut the door in his face."

She'd done exactly that, and she would have done it again if they had reapproached with that number. They'd lowballed the initial offering, hoping she was stupid. She wasn't. "The original offer was deserving of that, I believe."

"It was too low, and I apologize for that," the man said. He looked honest, but Josie had found out the hard way that honesty should never be taken at face value, and despite this guy's classic good looks—tall, broad-shouldered, curly light brown hair and blue eyes—she wasn't going to be fooled this time, either. Or ever again.

"I wasn't in on the initial negotiations," he continued. "If I had been, the offer would have been quite different. But fighting over this corner property has made for costly delays..."

"And has negatively affected your client's bottom line." Josie pretended to yawn. "I've read the briefs and you've gotten the county to side with you, so why is Carrington sending another lawyer to my door? You won. I have to dismantle my business and move, and while that's nothing to bigwigs like you, it's a huge deal to small-town businesspeople like me. Take your celebration elsewhere. We're closed."

The man withdrew a card from the pocket of his suit. "I'm not a lawyer. I'm Jacob Weatherly, the project manager for Carrington Hotels." He turned as a car door clicked shut from the parking area, and then he smiled. When he did, he looked almost human, which meant Josie was less likely to kick him in the shins for being on the winning team.

And then her heart stopped.

It didn't pause. It didn't skip. It came to a full-on stop as a strawberry blonde little girl came around the corner.

Adeline.

She stared at the girl, certain she must be seeing things. It had been three years, after all. Surely this child couldn't be—

"Come here, Addie-cakes." The man, Jacob Weatherly, put out a hand. "Was it getting warm in the car?"

The child shook her head. "I mostly wanted to see the big cow," she answered softly. She aimed a cautious look at Josie and had no idea what that look did to Josie's heart. "Why do you have such a big cow on your building? It's kind of funny, isn't it?"

Josie stared, unable to speak. Kimberly

jumped in to help. "They serve barbecue here. Barbecued beef and pork and chicken."

The girl nodded, but it was clear that she didn't get the correlation, and that was probably a good thing. How does one explain meat eating to an impressionable child? Josie had no idea.

"So you like cows?" The child sounded excited by the thought of Josie liking cows, and seeing her delight, Josie was sure she could make herself like cows. "I do, too! Daddy said we'd get a cow someday, when we settle someplace, but I don't really think that's going to happen. Is it, Daddy?" She peered up at Jacob Weatherly before reaching up to grasp his hand. "Because his job moves him around all the time."

Daddy?

Josie's brain whipped through what she knew about her biological daughter's adoptive parents. She'd kept the original information minimal on purpose, because she understood herself quite well. She wasn't the "open adoption" kind of mother. If she knew where Adeline was, she'd have been watching from a distance all this time. As it was, when Josie was needed to save the child's life, Addie's adoptive mother had found her.

But then Josie had purposely slipped into the shadows again, moving back north to Grace

Haven, avoiding the South on purpose. Only now, the South had come to her.

She swallowed hard. Brought a hand to her throat. It was no use. Words escaped her, which was probably a good thing because no one knew what had happened in Louisiana… and if Josie Gallagher had her way, no one ever would.

"Ms. Gallagher."

"Yes?" She pulled her attention from the beautiful child and faced Jacob Weatherly with more than real estate consternation in her stance.

Who was this man? How did he get Adeline? And how did he end up here, virtually next door to her seized property?

Questions raced through her brain, questions with no answers, but once she was alone she'd hunt for information. While the county might have the right to seize her business, her land and her lakefront footage without her permission…no one had the right to pass a child around in similar fashion.

"I know this isn't my place, but since development is my specialty, I looked around the lake at possible new venues for your restaurant."

Talk about salt in the wound. She flinched because here was a stranger with her child, trying to exert influence over her business life after his firm emerged victoriously from her lawsuit. Her pulse spiked. So did her blood pressure. And still, she couldn't speak. Or maybe she didn't dare speak.

"We don't want hard feelings, Ms. Gallagher." He held out his card again. "That's not how I do business. It's not how I ever do business. Please believe that."

Sincerity marked his gaze. He seemed to be totally up-front and earnest, but she'd fallen for that once, nearly seven years ago, and she'd vowed to never fall for it again.

Believe him?

Her gut quivered. Her fingers went cold, then hot, then cold again. Her palms became damp, but she ignored all of that and accepted the card because it would be her first step in finding out who Jacob Weatherly was and why Adeline was with him... And why did she call him "Daddy" when her adoptive father and mother were Ginger and Adam O'Neill from Georgia?

The only reason she knew that much was because when Addie needed a liver transplant at Emory, Josie'd flown up from New Orleans and donated the life-saving tissue to her beautiful child. She clasped the card, then slipped it into the back pocket of her jeans as if it wasn't the least bit important. "I appreciate the olive branch, Mr. Weatherly." She should have stopped there.

She couldn't.

She looked down into the sweetest sea-green eyes she'd ever seen. The tone had grown richer with time, giving Addie beautiful eyes, pale skin and hair that shone like a brand-new penny, much like her grandmother's. She looked so much like Cissy Gallagher that Josie was surprised Kimberly didn't notice. Maybe all freckled redheads looked alike?

But they didn't, and Addie was special. She'd known that from the beginning, reason enough right there to give the child a clean start at life. Twice. "Nice to meet you, Addie."

The girl offered a simple smile, the kind you'd offer a stranger. Josie's heart broke more, because in a perfect world, her daughter would recognize her birth mother and come running.

But in a world rife with adult problems, it was better for children to be protected and beloved, and as soon as everyone left her alone, she was going to find out why the project manager from Carrington Hotels had her daughter in his care.

Jacob Weatherly faced the frustrated restaurant owner in front of him and wished he'd been on hand when Carrington presented its first purchase offer. They'd misjudged this woman, and it was a foolish mistake made by people who thought they were better than the small business owners making up a huge percentage of America's workforce. They were wrong on that. Making enemies of the locals was a stupid thing to do.

She brought her gaze up from Addie and tried to hide the intensity of her emotions.

Atypical beauty.

The realization caught him off guard because he hadn't had time to notice women in a while. Being a single dad had changed his personal landscape. It had been a pretty big surprise, but the bigger surprise was how much he loved this child who'd already been through so much.

No more, though. He'd see to it that Addie's life was fairy-tale sweet from this point forward, although he wasn't sure how he could manage the cow she seemed determined to get.

"If you need me, my number and email are on the card. It's my cell phone." He tapped his jacket pocket. "So you don't have to go through automated prompts. I'd be happy to share the information I found at your convenience, Ms. Gallagher."

"I'm pretty sure you understand that nothing about this whole deal has been convenient." She faced him straight on, shoulders back, chin up.

High cheekbones said there might be Native American blood mixed with her Celtic name. "But I think I'd like to hear what you have to say, Mr. Weatherly."

She didn't want to hear him out. He saw that instantly, but she'd conceded. Why?

He had no idea, but if she thought she might be able to talk him out of taking over the land, she was wrong, and she seemed too smart to haggle over a done deal. "I'll wait for your call."

She gave him a curt nod, then glanced down at Addie.

Her gaze softened. She smiled at the six-year-old and squatted slightly. "A pleasure to meet you, Addie."

"Thank you." Addie pressed into his leg slightly, a touch shy, but only a touch, and she proved that right then by leaning forward, toward Josie Gallagher. "I think you might like my daddy a very lot, actually."

Josie's brows lifted quickly. "You think so?" She sounded more astounded than simply surprised.

"He's very nice." Addie pressed forward a little more, as if sharing a secret. "And he likes to go out with pretty ladies."

"Does he, now?" The striking woman pierced him with a sharp gaze, and he leaped to his own defense, then wondered why he felt compelled to do so.

"I don't. Addie Rose Weatherly, you're going to get me into trouble one of these days."

The girl giggled and grabbed him around the leg. "Well, silly, how are we going to find you a wife if you never ask pretty ladies to come see us? I don't think that's how it works, Dad."

"I'll find my own dates, thank you." He kept his tone dry, but when Addie burst out laughing, he had no choice. He reached down, picked her up, and marveled at how beautifully strong and healthy she was after such a rocky beginning. "Now say goodbye to these nice ladies. I've got a meeting at three, and I can't be late."

"Goodbye." She flashed the ladies a grin while she hugged him, and if he didn't know any better, he was pretty sure he'd been blessed beyond belief the day this little lady came into his life. She was the bright light in a sea of mourning. She made every day fuller and happier. He'd never thought about settling down and having children, and when his sister's marriage fell apart, he was pretty sure he'd made the right choice. Now, as he held the niece who was now his adopted daughter in his arms, Jacob was 100 percent certain he'd never have it any other way.

He settled Addie into the backseat of the

SUV, watched while she adjusted her shoulder strap, and when she snapped it to show him she'd tightened it correctly, he high-fived her. He'd just climbed into his seat when she surprised him from her perch. "Why was that lady mad at you?"

He could pretend that Josie Gallagher wasn't mad, but he'd be lying, and he never lied. "My company is buying her land and she has to move and she didn't want to move."

"You're making her move?" Surprise hiked Addie's gaze to his.

"Well…" He backed up, turned the car around and aimed for the two-lane road. "I'm not. But she has to move, yes."

"But you're building the new big place," she said reasonably. "So it's *like* you're making her move."

It was kind of like that, so he nodded, but wasn't happy to do it.

"And I get to go to big-kid school soon!"

Not much fazed Addie, and he loved that about her. They'd moved twice as he followed huge projects up the East Coast, and Addie seemed to find happiness wherever they landed, although now it was different. She was different. She was older and in need of schooling, and he was pushed to make some hard decisions about life and career. She needed roots, and after running projects on the fly for a dozen years, he might need some, too.

A boat horn sounded across the water as the *Canandaigua Lady* completed a lunchtime cruise. Bits of color tipped the trees, hinting new leaves. Daffodils and tulips brightened the landscapes surrounding the water, and the grass had gone from dull sage to kelly green in the past week. Spring was surging, and he had three months left on the Eastern Shore Inn project. By mid-July the project would be complete, and then what?

He wasn't tired of building. He loved putting jobs together, and he loved being a dad, two things he'd have never predicted as a younger man.

But since Addie came to him, he'd grown tired of pulling up stakes every few seasons.

He turned onto the road, and glanced back at the two women.

The taller one had moved forward and put an arm around Josie Gallagher, but Josie Gallagher wasn't looking at her friend.

She was watching him pull away, and the sorrowed look on her face made him want to pause. Turn back. Find out what was really wrong, what put that deepened sadness in her gaze.

He did no such thing. He had a business to

run for the next few months, and she was facing changes she didn't want or need, but they weren't his fault.

"She looks sad, doesn't she, Daddy?"

Right now he wished his beautiful daughter wasn't so intuitive. "Everybody gets sad sometimes, Addie-cakes."

"A little sad," she agreed, but when he glanced back, his daughter's troubled gaze was on the beautiful woman standing outside her soon-to-be-demolished restaurant. "But I think she's not just a little sad, Daddy. I think her heart hurts, like mine does sometimes."

What could he say to that? To have a father walk out because parenthood dragged him down, and then lose a mother to a tragic accident within months of Addie being declared cancer-free?

Addie had known heartache, and when foolish people reassured him she was too young to remember those early life tragedies, he bit his tongue to keep from lashing out.

He'd seen the grief in her little face and the naked sadness in her eyes. Time had eased much of that, but if Addie thought the Gallagher woman had a sore heart, he was inclined to believe it, because Addie had had way more experience with sadness than any six-year-old should ever have to face. No matter what he did, or what choices he made, from this point on he was totally invested in making sure her life was as trouble-free as it could be. She'd been dumped by a drug-using birth mother, abandoned by an adoptive father, fought cancer and won, only to lose her mother in a commuter train crash.

Now she had him. And he had her. And with God on their side, they'd make everything work out. Despite Addie's funny attempts to gain him a wife, they were doing okay. And that was all right by him.

Chapter Two

"Josie."

Josie didn't want to make eye contact with Kimberly, but her cousin's proximity left her little choice. "Yes?"

"What's going on?"

Josie moved toward the restaurant side of the building. "Change is in the air, it seems. I need to make a list."

Kimberly's hand on her arm made her pause, but not because she wanted to. With Kimberly's due date so close, she didn't want to be a jerk, but seeing Addie had rattled her entire being.

Her restaurant gone, her beautiful daughter climbing out of a strange man's car and the secret she'd buried seven long years ago yawning widely… "It's just a lot to handle, Kimberly. I was hoping we'd win, that it wouldn't come to this." She splayed her hands in the direction of the barbecue joint. "And yet it did."

Kimberly studied her. She started to say something, then stopped herself. "We've been friends and cousins since we were born, Josie."

Josie nodded. They'd grown up hand in hand, then lost touch for a while, and now here they were, back in Grace Haven. Kimberly had found the love of her life. She had a great job, a lovely new home and a second baby on the way.

Josie had nothing, and that reality didn't sit well.

"Whatever it is, it might be easier to talk about it."

"There's nothing, Kimberly. Except losing all these years of work and effort, watching it get the wrecking ball and bury my hopes and dreams with it. Other than that, it's nothing much at all."

She wanted Kimberly to buy that story and let things go, but Kimberly arched one brow and then made a little face of regret. "I'll be here when you're ready."

Josie waved her off deliberately.

She had no intention of being ready, ever. She'd shoved that horrible night and the ensuing time into a deep, dark closet of her consciousness, and she kept it there, locked up tight. She'd moved through life making decisions in Addie's best interests…

But *were* those decisions still in her daughter's best interests? Because seeing her with a stranger and calling him "Dad" sparked too many mental red flags. She couldn't research any of this with Kimberly around, so she kept her emotions at bay and her hands steady. "I just need time, Kimberly. That's all. Time to get used to this."

Unconvinced, Kimberly moved to her car. Josie followed, and when Kimberly turned and hugged her goodbye, Josie longed to spill her guts, but didn't. She'd kept the secret for so long already. What use would revealing it do? But could she keep it to herself with Addie living so close?

The thought of her daughter nearby sobered her more.

What would that mean? Would she have to move away from the family and friends who'd helped build her business and her self-esteem over the years she'd spent here? How long would the Weatherly man be in Grace Haven?

The host of questions with no answers would hound her until she had time to do more research, and as Kimberly released her, a big part of Josie wanted to tell her everything.

But she'd promised herself and her baby

daughter that no one would ever know about the crime associated with Addie's conception. What child should ever have to grow up knowing that?

None.

She waited for Kimberly to pull away, and moved back to the apartment. She retrieved her laptop from a dusty shelf, opened it, typed in her password and then began a search. One way or another she was going to find out what had happened to her beautiful child in the past few years, and Josie Gallagher was pretty sure she wasn't going to like any of it.

Josie stared at the Peachtree City obituary for Ginger O'Neill and fought the rise of emotion. Addie's adoptive mother had died in an accident involving a commuter train. That was tragic enough, but there was no husband listed in the obituary, and no father for Addie. Ginger was survived by her parents and one brother, Jacob Weatherly.

Addie was being raised by her adoptive uncle.

Where was the father who signed all the paperwork to legally adopt her? Where was Adam O'Neill? And how could Josie find out without looking like a stalker? Regret grabbed hold and wouldn't let go.

When she'd arrived in Georgia to be a living

donor transplant for Addie, she'd seen Ginger. Not Adam. Was he already out of the picture at that time? When Ginger said Adam was too emotional to meet with Josie, she'd believed her. But maybe that wasn't the truth?

She lifted her phone and dialed Drew Slade, Kimberly's husband and the chief of police for Grace Haven. He answered quickly and she dived right in. "I need advice, Drew."

"Mine to give," he answered. "What's up?"

"I can't talk over the phone. Can I come by? Or can you stop out here?"

"I'm heading home around four, so how about I swing over there first?"

"Yes. Thank you. And Drew..." He waited at the other end until she continued. "I can't talk about this to anyone else right now. It's got to be private. Okay?"

"Meaning don't tell Kimberly because you know she'll go ballistic?"

The thought of her family knowing how stupid she'd been...after she'd vowed to never be stupid again...

Her heart ached at the thought of disappointing people she loved, but worse, how could she mess up the innocence of a child who'd already gone through so much? "I'll explain in person, but I might need your help looking into someone, making sure he's a good person."

"I'll be there at four. And Josie?"

"Yes?"

"Whatever is bothering you, we'll make it right. I promise. Okay?"

He had no idea what he was saying because as good and strong as Drew was, no one could ever make this okay, and she'd known that from the beginning. "See you later."

She hung up the phone, grabbed her keys and drove a quarter mile south. The construction road leading to the new waterfront hotel was blocked. Jacob Weatherly had mentioned a three o'clock meeting. It was two thirty-five right now. She crossed through the construction tape, ignored the shouts of a couple of guys in hard hats and circled the newly finished concrete sidewalk rimming the stately hotel base. She pulled out her cell phone to call Jacob Weatherly, then nearly ran into him as she rounded the corner of the hotel.

"Hi!" Addie jumped up on the sculpted concrete edge of a raised garden and waved. "You came to find us!"

Addie looked excited to see Josie. Jacob Weatherly's expression was more guarded. "Did you just walk through a hard hat area without permission?"

"I needed to see you." She held his gaze, almost daring him to read more into the situation. "You said you had ideas on my relocation. I'd like to hear more about them, and I'm right up the beach, as you know." She glanced north to emphasize the proximity. "But the beach is blocked off and the only way into this complex right now is by the road."

"And permission." He assessed her with a thoughtful look. "You had my number."

She held up her phone. "I was just about to call you."

"I see." He breathed deeply, as if thinking, then took Addie's hand. "I've got a meeting in a few minutes, so I can't discuss this now, but if you'd like, I can come by tomorrow morning. How does nine o'clock sound?"

"Like breakfast time, and I make a marvelous French toast with fresh fruit and whipped cream." She smiled down at Addie when she said it, and should have felt ashamed for enticing the girl, but she didn't. Not even a little bit. Seeing Addie well and healthy after fighting cancer gave Josie a lift to her spirits, but deepened her concerns.

Had the O'Neills lied in their adoption application? What happened to Adam? Her preliminary internet search turned up nothing, so wherever he was, and whatever he was doing, it wasn't out there for public viewing.

"We can have breakfast before we come

over." The project manager lifted his watch to show his diminishing time frame.

"But I love strawberries and French toast so much, Dad." Addie tipped back her head and implored him with a beseeching look while thick copper curls spilled across the shoulders of her long-sleeved T-shirt. "And I'll be so good!"

"There is a reason why my restaurant was voted number one in Southern fare and barbecue for two years running," Josie noted. "And I've got a few supplies I need to use up before the move." She left the offer sensible. If she pushed too hard, he might get suspicious. Clearly he had no idea about her relationship to the child clutching his hand. For now, she'd keep it that way.

"She does love French toast."

Addie wrung his hand, grinning.

"All right, nine o'clock for breakfast. Although…" He turned her way again with a questioning expression. "I'm surprised, Miss Gallagher. And surprises raise questions in my head. I'm sure you can understand that, especially when your relationship with my employer has been adversarial." He held her gaze, and Josie refused to blink or quiver. "But let's see what tomorrow brings."

"Perfect." She turned to go, and he caught her hand.

Instant panic set in.

Her heart rate soared. Her hands went cold and her feet refused to move.

He didn't seem to notice as he directed her to the small parking area alongside the finished portion of the hotel. "Let me drive you to your car so the outdoor crew doesn't go ballistic on you. They'd catch the boss's fury if he thought you were walking in dangerous areas without proper gear. You might not like too much about Carrington Hotels right now, but there's a reason they've been voted one of the top ten construction companies in the country, and that's because they care about quality and safety. That's part of the reason I've been with them for a dozen years," he added. He released her hand to open both doors on the passenger side. "Quality and safety are top on my radar, too."

She shelved the bits of information he was giving her. She'd give them to Drew when he came by, but as she climbed into the front seat of Jacob Weatherly's car, their hands touched again, briefly.

This touch spurred no panic. Was that because she read the gentleness in his gaze? The humor he slanted back, toward Addie, as she made a big show about getting her seat belt buckled? Or was it the honesty she discerned in his face?

You've been fooled before. Don't let it happen again.

She took the mental warning to heart because she'd made a grievous mistake once. She'd fallen for the winning smile and trusted the wrong man.

Right now, with Addie living there in her neighborhood, she couldn't afford to make a mistake again. She'd entrusted two people with her most precious possession, her newborn child. What happened after that was anyone's guess, but she was determined to get to the bottom of it, because Addie deserved what Josie had promised her: a nice, normal life, unblemished by scandal. Josie had every intention of making sure her daughter got exactly that.

Strong, yet scared. Or maybe *scarred* was a better word, Jacob mused as he pulled up next to Josie's aging SUV a few moments later. He'd noticed the two catering trucks in her side parking lot, brilliantly bright and absolutely clean. Her restaurant had a similar appearance, while rugged enough to be a classic dive. She'd captured the retro look outside. Tomorrow morning would give him a look inside the Bayou Barbecue. The legal battle had kept him from stopping by before now. Carrington lawyers didn't want anything muddying the waters of eminent domain. Now he'd get to see the internal workings of the east shore go-to spot for great food.

Josie swung her door open and got out of the car quickly. "Thanks for the ride." The look she gave him was pleasant but probably insincere. Understandable after his company had seized her land.

Then she looked toward Addie, and it was nothing but pure warmth and joy. "I'm going to go get the berries right now, so we're all ready for tomorrow morning. Okay?"

Addie clasped her hands together. "Okay!"

She stepped back and shut the door. Jacob pulled away and headed for the work trailer offices behind the chain-link fencing. He glanced back, through the rearview mirror.

Josie had gotten into her car and was backing out of the space. He found that reassuring for some reason. Her surprise arrival concerned him. She'd shown up, out of the blue. She'd crossed a construction zone. She—he paused and his thoughts took a different route, a more personal one.

She was downright beautiful, and clearly worried. Who wouldn't be in her situation?

As he pulled up to the double-wide work

trailer, Addie leaped out of her seat and waved toward the road.

Josie Gallagher was driving by. She spotted the girl and gave a quick wave back, nothing over the top, but it seemed to make Addie happy. "I like her, Daddy!"

She clutched his hand and skipped alongside as he approached the work trailer. "You do?"

"Mmm-hmm." She bobbed her head and her curls bounced. "She has really pretty hair."

He couldn't fault her six-year-old reasoning because he'd noticed Josie's hair, too. Dark brown, with copper-red highlights, but not enough to be called auburn. And those smoke-toned eyes with a hint of green. He'd noticed their odd shade as she turned the corner of the concrete walk and their eyes met.

"I would love a dolly with hair like that," Addie confessed. "All of my dolls have hair like mine." She sighed as if hair made a difference. It didn't, of course. "I might be really, really tired of yellow hair."

"Strawberry blond," he reminded her and laid a hand over her head. "Really pretty strawberry blond hair, and I think you're exactly the way God wanted you to be, Addie-cakes."

"Well, I don't think he'd mind if I had a brown-haired dolly." The logic of her reasoning wasn't lost on him. "I think he'd be okay with that, actually."

He'd never really noticed that her dolls were all light-haired. A couple were from her early years, and several were more recent gifts, but she was right. Every one of them was pale and blond-or copper-haired. Clearly he and his parents thought alike, but that was shortsighted. Her playthings should have diversity, shouldn't they? To reflect the real world?

He set up Addie with a juice box and crackers in the front room, then arranged for the conference call in the adjacent office. He made a note to check out the doll situation when he had time, then refocused his attention on dock-building bids. For the moment, Addie would have to get by with what she had with her, and she was such an easygoing child, he was sure that would be just fine.

"You never told anyone about the attack?" She'd surprised Drew Slade, Josie realized less than two hours later, and a man who used to be top security for the current president of the United States didn't surprise easily. "Josie, why not? They could have helped you. They still could," he added firmly.

Fear and shame had held her tongue seven years ago. She clenched her hands in her lap and wondered how all of her careful reasoning had come to this. "I wasn't on the best terms with my family when I went to Louisiana."

"How so?"

"Kimberly never told you?" That made her feel better, somehow. Not that she wanted Kimberly to keep secrets from Drew, but she was glad her stupid mistakes hadn't become gossip fodder.

Drew shook his head.

"I messed up in college. Big-time. I cut loose, and partied with all the wrong people after my Dad died. I flunked out midway through my sophomore year and became a bitter disappointment to the Gallagher clan."

"We all make mistakes," Drew replied. "I'm a card-carrying member of Alcoholics Anonymous myself, so I hear you. But I don't get what one has to do with the other."

"I embarrassed my family, and they worked hard to help me get straightened out," she told him. "Counseling, rehab and a job. They stuck by me despite what I did. When I decided I wanted to work the barbecue circuit in the Deep South, my mother and aunts tried to talk me out of it because there's plenty of temptation in New Orleans. For a barbecue cook, though, it is the place to be if you want to learn all the aspects of good Southern cooking."

"You moved down there anyway."

She sighed. "Even though they asked me not to. New Orleans is too wild, they said. My mother begged me to stay home, or to go to some other Southern city, but anyone who is anyone in the barbecue business does a stint in New Orleans. And I was stubborn."

Drew's grunt indicated he understood that part well enough. Of course, he was married to a Gallagher, so he had firsthand experience.

"I was there for over two years with no problems, and learning all kinds of things. I got a chance to work with Big Bobby and Tuck Fletcher and Cajun Mary, so I learned from the best. And then this guy shows up—he starts flirting with me and it's all in fun." She frowned and gripped her knees tighter. "He seemed so normal, and I'd let my radar down because I'd been on the straight-and-narrow path for a long time. I'd forgotten how slick some guys can be. He was going to meet me for dinner, but then he called and said his car stalled near the parking lot of my apartment complex and it would be a while for them to tow it. Could he come up and wait? I said sure." She bit her lip, remembering. "He slipped something into my glass of tea. When I woke up the next morning, he was gone."

Drew didn't just look mad. He looked furious. "Why didn't you call it in? The guy's a criminal."

If Josie could have tucked her chin any deeper into her shirt, she would have, but it was impossible. "I couldn't face those inquiries. And if they caught him and brought him to trial, then I'd have to face how stupid I was in college. They bring up everything, you know. They'd have brought up my past, and made it public knowledge. They shouldn't, but they do." She raised her eyes and faced Drew candidly. "I couldn't go through all that again. I'd come so far. I just wanted to put it behind me. For the whole stupid thing to be over."

"But it wasn't."

A tear slipped down her cheek. She dashed it away, but not before another one joined the first. "Three weeks later, I discovered I was pregnant."

Drew had been jotting things down. He stopped.

"I had a little girl no one knows about. Her name is Addie. Adeline," she added. "I worked with a very nice agency down there. I was determined that my child would have the best possible chance at life. I wanted her to grow up untarnished by the circumstances surrounding her creation. No child deserves to have that kind of baggage weighing them down, do they?"

"No. Of course not. The agency arranged everything?"

She nodded. "I wanted a closed adoption so I wouldn't be tempted to check up on things, but I said I could be contacted for life-and-death situations. Two and a half years later, I was contacted by the adoptive mother, Ginger O'Neill. Addie had tumors on her liver. She needed a transplant and they couldn't find a good match. They tested me and I was a match. I pretended I was taking a winter vacation from the restaurant. I flew to Emory, had the procedure done and saved Addie's life."

"All with no one knowing what was going on. That must have been incredibly difficult to go through alone." Drew sat back. "You're an amazing woman, Josie."

She held up her hands, palms out, to stop him from saying more. "I did what any mother would do. But here's the problem, Drew. The project manager for the Carrington Hotel going up next door? He has my daughter with him."

"Here?"

Josie nodded, grimly "He came over here today to offer advice, and Addie climbed out of his car."

"A lot of kids look alike, Josie."

She handed over her phone with the obituary page highlighted. "Her mother died. Her adoptive father is out of the picture, but I don't know how or why. This uncle, Jacob Weatherly, has my daughter with him and I need to know what's going on because a child isn't like a piece of real estate. They're not a commodity to be bargained with or handed around. They're people, and the deal I struck with the adoption agency and the O'Neills has been broken."

"Don't get ahead of yourself, here."

She stuck out her chin, stubborn as ever.

"Once an adoption is finalized, it's done. So if something happened to the parents, then they have the right to assign a guardian in their absence. Are you worried that this is a bad guy? Did he hurt her? Or seem mean?"

"Just the opposite, but that's not the point, Drew."

His expression said it might be the point, even if she didn't agree with it.

"She was mine first."

"Yes. But the legal agreement between you and the agency—"

"Is binding," she interrupted. "But what if the adoptive father misrepresented himself? I checked all over the internet and couldn't find a thing about him, except a divorce record filed two months after the adoption was finalized."

Drew sat back. "You think he never intended to stay married while they were adopting Addie?"

"That's exactly what I think. And I think his wife knew that, because she lied about him when I came to Emory. She made excuses for why he wasn't there, why she was taking care of everything. I didn't put it together at the time, but looking back I see the pattern. I know I signed away my rights to my daughter, and I did that willingly, to give her a fresh start. But if the O'Neills were acting out a role so that Ginger could have a child, even though she knew her husband wasn't interested in having a child, that's fraud."

"It could be. But this isn't exactly my expertise, Josie. Cruz is more schooled in law than I am, and he'd know who to contact."

"I agree. But what I need from you is more immediate while I check out the legal sides of all of this. I need you to check up on Jacob Weatherly. I know his sister lied to me. He seems nice on the surface, and he was sweet to Addie, but I'm done taking chances, Drew. I've been living a lie for seven years, trying to protect her—"

"And yourself, maybe?"

She couldn't deny it. "That, too, but mostly I wanted a solid life for her. I did all the right things, Drew, and it still came out all wrong. Now we need to fix it." She didn't have to read his expression to know it wasn't that easy. "I don't know how we can make this right, but the first thing we need to do is to run a check on this new adoptive father. Can you do that for me?"

"I've got a few connections." Drew stood. "I'll take care of it. But Josie, when are you going to tell the family what happened? When will you open up to them?"

"I don't know." She bit her lower lip and shook her head. "I guess I'll have to, won't I?"

"Yes."

"I need time." She spoke softly. "I've spent all these years keeping this secret, a little more time can't hurt. But I can't rest easy until I know she's in good hands for the time being."

"Consider it done. And then?"

And then…she had no idea, but the thought that a married couple would pretend to be happy to gain a child, and then split up once they had her…

She felt deceived, and she was pretty sure they'd deceived the adoption agency, too, which meant the agency had a stake in this convoluted situation. But Addie came first. She walked Drew to the door. "I don't know what will happen next. I can't leave it like this, with all these loose ends. I wanted Addie's childhood to be wonderful. If I'd known that Ginger would be raising her alone, I'd have picked another couple. The agency had a whole book of them. It's not because I'm controlling, but it was the most important decision I've ever had to make. If they misrepresented their marriage, that's a huge thing."

He hugged her.

The embrace felt good. She was relieved to have finally told someone the truth. When he released her, he stepped back and pointed north, toward the village of Grace Haven. "You need to tell them. All of them. I won't say a word, but once Cruz gets someone to check out the legal end of things, word could spread, and you don't want your mother or the rest of the family finding out accidentally. Gossip spreads fast in small towns."

It did. "I'll figure it out. And I won't wait too long. I have to get used to the idea first. You probably think I was pretty stupid back then. Don't you?"

He shook his head instantly. "You did nothing wrong. You feel stupid because you trusted the wrong person, but that doesn't make you stupid, Josie. It makes him a criminal." His quick rebuttal and strong voice lent strength to his reply. "I'd like to get my hands on him and let him know that defending a woman's honor hasn't gone out of style."

His words bolstered her. Tears smarted her eyes again, because the thought of someone sticking up for her seemed wonderful, but shamed her, too. Her family probably would have reacted like this. Just like this. And she hadn't given them the chance. If she had—

"Stop second-guessing yourself, and I'll let you know what I find," he ordered. "And get hold of Cruz quickly. We need to know where we stand legally. He'll know who to contact about that. If the original adoption was fraudulent, that could negate any subsequent court rulings because they rested on the assumption that the initial adoption was legitimate."

She hated the thought of Addie being bound up in legal proceedings, but she couldn't think only of that. She had to think of what had happened in the past, and how that had affected a child's life. "I'll talk to him tomorrow." She started to step back, but Drew put his hands on her shoulders and held her attention.

"I'm glad you finally told someone. There's a reason the Bible says the truth shall set you free. Because it's true."

The Bible spoke of truth often. The good book was a champion of honesty and integrity and sacrifice, all the reasons she'd sought a solid, happy couple to raise her child because she didn't want Addie fettered with a dark beginning. From what she could see now, the adoption had thrust Addie into a different dark beginning, and that wasn't fair to the child or the birth mother. One way or another, she needed to fix it.

Chapter Three

Jacob pulled into the parking lot adjacent to the Bayou Barbecue and thought hard before going in. Neutral ground would have been a smarter choice, considering Carrington's winning stance. Agreeing to this breakfast meeting might have been a mistake. He could easily take Addie into the Grace Haven Diner for French toast, forget about breakfast with Josie Gallagher and reschedule their meeting. He was about to do that when she stepped outside the restaurant door.

"Hi!" Addie yelled the greeting with bright enthusiasm before he made good on his escape plan. She set her picture book aside and unlatched her shoulder strap quickly. In a flash she was out the door. "I'm so glad we're here, I love French toast with syrup, and with powdery sugar, and with fruit and with, oh…" She beamed up at the woman with shining eyes, as if she'd just spotted a long-lost friend. "I like your pretty brown hair."

Josie Gallagher bent low and smiled right at Addie, the way someone did when they were good with kids. "You want the truth?"

Addie nodded, still excited. "Yes!"

"I always wanted coppery hair, just like yours."

"No!" Addie put her hands on her hips and offered the Gallagher woman a look of total surprise. "Are you kidding me?"

Josie shook her head, smiling. "Not even a little bit."

"Because I was just telling my dad that I wanted a dolly or maybe even two dollies with dark hair like yours. All my dolls have this color." She pulled a strand of hair to the right and sighed. "I want some dolls with different hair. Like yours. Or maybe Dad's hair."

"Brown with gray accents?" He laughed as he drew closer. "That would be a strange mix for a baby doll, wouldn't it?"

"Not the gray, silly, and I think your hair is perfect, Dad. Just like you."

His heart melted. He could be tough as needed, and if he thought she was simply buttering him up for a new toy or adventure, he wasn't afraid to say no. He'd learned by watching his overly indulged sister that life should be lived with some limits, even if the requests were affordable. But Addie wasn't pulling a con job on him. She loved him, and that had to be the best feeling of all. "Well, thank you. I think you're pretty spectacular too, kid." He lifted a small binder into the air. "I brought some ideas, Miss Gallagher."

"Josie, please."

He hesitated and briefly wasn't sure why, but then it clicked. She'd been ready to give him the heave-ho yesterday, less than twenty-four hours ago. Had she undergone a change of heart? Or was there another reason behind her friendlier gestures? And if so, what was it?

He wasn't sure, but he didn't want to be rude. "And I'm Jacob." He reached out a hand. "Maybe it would be good if we started all over again. What do you say?"

She took his hand and looked right at him. "I think that's a good idea. Nice to meet you, Jacob."

"You guys are silly!" Addie planted her hands on her hips again, a newly acquired habit from one of her favorite TV shows. "You already met yesterday. Me, too!"

"So we did." Jacob ruffled her hair with his hand. "But sometimes grown-ups need a do-over. Just like kids do."

"Like me and Cayden at school. Except he's not very nice, and I might not give him any more do-overs. Because he should be nice, shouldn't he, Dad?"

"Yes. But it is good to give people another chance," he added. "Although I'm not sure how many is too many in preschool."

"I'm in kindergarten, Dad. Kindergarten is not preschool!"

He grimaced. "My bad." He faced Josie. "She's been going to the Lakeside Academy, where they move from preschool to kindergarten before they go to public school. It seemed smart with my job."

"Except this year, I get to go to regular school and we just have to figure out where." Addie turned earnest eyes his way. "And get a cow."

"We're not getting a cow, Addie-cakes. It won't fit in the car. Or the apartment." He grinned to show her he was kidding, but Addie had grown very serious about two things: school and settling down with a cow.

"When we get a big yard, a cow will fit." She didn't sass him. She didn't act petulant. She uttered the sentence with a quiet common sense far beyond her years, and then she grabbed his hand. At that moment, her stomach gurgled and she laughed. "My tummy is so hungry now! Miss Josie, can I see your restaurant? How come there aren't any people here? Did they all go home?"

Her innocent question made Jacob's stomach lurch. He and Carrington Hotels were the reason her place was closed. He waited for her to throw him under the bus, but Josie surprised him.

"We're moving my restaurant to another spot, and I need a little time to pack things up. It's hard to cook and pack at the same time, right?"

"Oh, that's right." Addie lifted an empathetic look to Josie. "My dad is making you move."

He started to protest, but Josie beat him to it. She bent low. "Well, he works for a company that needs more space. So the company is taking my space, and giving me money to move somewhere new. That's why your dad is here, because he's got some ideas about how to help me." The quiet and up-front way she handled Addie was somewhat unexpected and allowed him to breathe easier.

"We can eat and talk." Addie grasped his hand with hers. "Dad always says we should help other people, all the time. I mostly do that, but I don't like helping Cayden when he's mean."

"Well, school's almost over for the year,"

Jacob said. "That will solve our Cayden problems."

"I'm glad," Addie said.

"I think some of this French toast will take our minds off snippy boys." Josie led the way inside. "Give me five minutes in the kitchen, okay? Or you can follow me in there, but you have to sit on the bar stools."

"You don't mind?" Jacob asked, and when she lifted her eyes to his, he got a little lost in the depths, as if he and Josie Gallagher were connected in some way he didn't understand.

The odd mix of colors seemed more gold today than green, but the shadow of gray rimming the pupil seemed lighter than it had yesterday. And when she smiled, the gray thinned even more. "I don't mind a bit. I like for kids to see what goes on in a kitchen, although if it was still a working kitchen, we couldn't do this often. It got crazy here on a regular basis."

"I've heard that. And I hope you don't mind, but I fact-checked your numbers, Josie."

She accepted that as she heated the broad, flat griddle in the kitchen. "I figured Carrington did that before they drew up an offer, and it only makes sense for you to know the facts if we're talking location. The thing is…"

She dipped thick slices of cinnamon swirl bread into a custardy mix and set them sizzling onto the hot griddle before checking a warming kettle of strawberry topping. "There are few available locations on the water, and most are unaffordable. I fell into this location because the former owner let things go and needed help. We worked out a deal and it ended up being a success for both of us, but as you've seen—"

She paused as she turned a pan of flat, deliciously scented sausage patties with a flick of her wrist, a neat trick. "There's almost nothing available. I'm not sure what you've found, Jacob, but even with the Carrington money, it's probably unaffordable. And that was reason enough for me to dread this whole thing because it's not the starting over that concerns me." She moved the sausage to a platter, then nestled fresh, hot French toast onto three warm plates. "I've got the clientele and the reputation. Folks will follow me. But if I can't afford a lakeside place to own or rent, then it's all been for nothing. And that's what bites." She crossed to where Addie was perched, avidly watching the action. And when she slipped a platter of mouthwatering food in front of his daughter, Addie's eyes went wide.

"You've won her over." He made the comment casually as she brought the third plate over, but when Josie looked his way, she wasn't casual anymore. She looked intent. As if his words meant more than they did.

And then she sat down across from Addie and gave her an easy smile. "Well, that wasn't too hard."

Addie laughed and picked up a knife and fork. "Can I cut this by myself?"

Jacob nodded. "I expect, but if you need help, just let me know."

"Okay! And I think we should pray about this nice food, shouldn't we, Dad?" Addie leaned in and sniffed, then raised a brilliant smile his way. "We always pray at supper time, but why don't people just pray all the time? Like breakfast, lunch and supper? Doesn't that make the most sense of all?"

She reached out a hand to him on one side and Josie on the other. He did the same.

Soft hands, but not as smooth as someone who didn't do physical work, or plunge their hands into dish soap all day.

But soft, still. Strong. And beautiful. Like the woman sitting next to him. "Father, we thank you for this food. We ask your blessings on it and on us, Lord, as we go through our days. Amen."

"Amen."

"See?" Addie beamed his way, then shared the grin with Josie. "That wasn't even hard, was it? And now we made God's heart happy, because we remembered to pray."

"I won't forget again," he promised. He released her hand and Josie's, but when he looked at the woman beside him, her gaze was locked on Addie.

She smiled, yes, but tears brightened her eyes, as if seeing his daughter and hearing her delightfully colloquial speech touched her deeply.

Addie had sensed her pain. As he lifted his napkin into his lap, Jacob sensed the same thing again. But when she turned his way, she'd erased the look of angst. She smiled, glanced at Addie and said, "I expect she keeps you on your toes, Jacob."

"And then some." He watched as Addie attacked her French toast, and when she cut it sufficiently to eat, he turned back toward Josie. "And I wouldn't have it any other way. She's made my life the best it's ever been, and we've got a good thing going. At least until the whole issue of a cow came up." He made a face at Addie and she laughed.

"This is the best French toast I ever had, Miss Josie! And we've got time to get the cow, Dad. It's not even summer yet!"

Josie laughed. "She's tenacious."

"I'd go straight to stubborn, but tenacious

sounds better. Inside those china-doll good looks is an independent spirit with a heart of gold. Although I'm not sure how the whole cow thing started."

"With so many baby cows on the hills, Dad." Addie paused chewing and pointed across the lake. "Not by the grape things, but with the farmers. And one farmer has a ton of little black cows. They're the cutest things!"

"My cousin." Josie followed the direction of Addie's hand and met Jacob's gaze. "Bryan Gallagher has a combination crop-and-animal farm at the south end of the lake. Angus cows and a big, busy farm stand near the road. We could go visit sometime if she'd like to see the cows up close."

"Oh, can we, Dad? Can we? For real?"

Something made him long to say no, but how could he when Josie was making such a kind offer? Visiting cows wasn't exactly a bad thing. "Josie and I will check our calendars. But I don't see why we shouldn't go visit the cows. And then maybe you can kind of adopt one and pretend it's yours. What do you think, Josie?" He turned back to her. "Is your cousin open to bovine adoption?"

She winced, then tried to cover it with a smile. "Brian's got three kids of his own, so he probably understands this stuff way better than most. I'm sure he'd be fine with it, but I'd advise you to pick a female." She raised a brow to him, and after a few seconds, he got her gist.

"Easy enough because Addie already has a name picked out."

"You do?"

As Josie slanted her gaze to Addie, Jacob realized she hadn't really eaten with them. She'd only taken a bite or two while Addie had plowed through a piece of the thick, delicious toast, a bowl of warm berries and two sausage patties. She might be small but she had a trucker's appetite, and he couldn't fault her because the meal was delicious.

Addie started to grin, then realized she was chewing. "Polly," she told her once she'd swallowed and washed down the food with chilled orange juice. "Polly the cow. I think it's a good name for one, don't you?"

"It's a marvelous name. So." She swiveled on the stool back toward him. "I know you're busy, and I don't mean to take up too much time. If you have ideas, Jacob, I'd like to hear them."

"I do." He spoke cautiously, still wondering if he was doing the right thing, but then scolded himself. Offering her a spot couldn't be a bad idea, not with the reviews he'd read on the internet and the glowing reports from customers. Those were backed up by mighty impressive figures because new restaurants rarely succeeded. Hers had not only succeeded, but flourished in an area surrounded by busy chain restaurants in nearby plazas. And yet the Bayou Barbecue stood tall. "You were right about the lack of available waterfront."

She grimaced.

"But what would you say to a cooperative effort?"

The grimace turned to a quick frown.

"Carrington has given me the go-ahead to offer you premier restaurant space on the ground floor of the hotel, facing the north-end beach. It would have outdoor seating and gathering spots during the warm months, and indoor seating during the rest of the year, and a take-out shack."

She stared at him, then Addie, then him again. She swallowed hard, then brought a hand to her throat. "I could put the Bayou Barbecue there? In the hotel?"

"It makes sense to us for multiple reasons. First." He held up one finger. "We're taking your space, and this could be in your best interests because then you're virtually in the same location. A matter of beach frontage would be the only difference."

She held his gaze, listening.

"Second, you've got a successful business

you've worked hard to develop, and the hotel would love a beach-themed restaurant on the ground level. Why not yours? Why go outside the area for a chain when we've got top quality right here? And before you ask how I know that, your reviews and numbers have been checked thoroughly. You're not even a gamble for us, Josie. The Bayou Barbecue is the real deal, and we'd be stupid not to extend this offer."

"To put the restaurant in the hotel?" She made a face of consternation. "What about the locals? Could they access it? Where would they park? I don't want them to feel like they have to get dressed up to come get food."

"Casual, beachwear, flip-flops, totally dive-friendly. We'll even do the decor to reflect what you've got here, and if you'd throw your smokers into the deal, we'll move everything under your supervision and design the kitchen to your specifications with a July 1 opening date. The take-out shack would make it easy for folks to do drive-through like they do here, and we could have that staffed twelve months of the year if it's heated."

She should say no.

She should say no because to oversee the restaurant at the hotel, with Addie right there... How could she do this, then watch her leave in a few months? How could she put herself through that?

But then she looked over at her daughter's happy face, a face bearing her grandmother's sea-green eyes and pale, Celtic skin. The narrow dusting of powdered sugar around sweet pink lips cemented her answer, because looking at Addie, there really wasn't a choice. "I'd like that, Jacob. I'd like it a lot. How soon can you have the paperwork ready for me to run by my lawyer?"

He handed her the folder. "We were hoping you'd consider the idea."

Her heart went tight. Stark reality said she needed to hand back his folder and quietly walk away because of the deal she'd struck with the agency over six years before. But now—

Things were different now, and not by her doing. Something had gone wrong shortly after the adoption papers were filed, and if Ginger and Adam O'Neill had done that intentionally, they'd accepted Addie under fraudulent terms.

Josie wasn't sure how to set things right. She needed more information, and taking this rental contract to Cruz would give her the excuse to put him on the trail. But one way or another, the thought of working in the same area with her beloved daughter was too good a chance to pass up. "I like a company that plans ahead. I'll run these by my lawyer's office this afternoon and get back to you."

"By five o'clock Thursday?"

She nodded, stood and slipped the folder onto a stainless steel countertop. "Absolutely."

"Then we should go." He stood, too, and when Addie sighed, he angled his head. "Really? I brought you over for the best breakfast we've had in a long time, kid. Don't push it."

Addie didn't whine. She didn't pout. She slid down off the stool, then grabbed Josie in a hug—a hug she'd dreamed about for six long years. A hug that made her realize she would never want to let the girl go again...

"Thank you, Miss Josie! It was great!"

"You're welcome, Addie."

"And I'll look forward to hearing from you, Josie. If your lawyer offers approval before Thursday, just call me. I'll get a crew right over to dismantle everything and bring it up the beach."

Two months with Addie.

Two months watching the child she'd given away as she laughed, skipped and hopped her way through life.

She didn't need Cruz's approval for that. No matter the terms, she'd grab this contract because it offered her something she never thought she'd have, time with her daughter. And that was a dream come true, no matter what the terms.

Chapter Four

"Josie." Cruz Maldonado set the contract down on the upscale desktop. He bridged his hands, thoughtful. "This deal with Carrington looks fine. I've got a few tweaks to make, nothing they should balk at. But then we come to the other situation, your little girl…"

His words made her swallow hard.

No one ever talked about "her little girl," even when she was donating a life-giving organ. Everyone treated her as a kindly bene-factor, while Ginger had gotten all the sweet mother references. Josie had swallowed it like a bitter pill then, determined to save Addie's life, but hearing Cruz speak the phrase made it real.

She had a little girl. A precious child. Here. Now.

"I've got a friend in New York who special-izes in adoptions. I'm going to send the facts to her, and she'll have a team sort through it and find out what went wrong. She's got resources I can't access, and she's good. Rory and I used her to ensure everything went fine with Lily and Javi."

Lily and Javi were his cousin's orphaned children, two beautiful youngsters he and Rory had adopted months before.

"Life can be weird." When she frowned, Cruz raised a hand of caution. "Sometimes coincidental timing messes things up. But on first look, I have to agree with you. The timing sounds contrived, and while it's unfortunate, it's nothing that hasn't been done before, according to my friend. She described it as an upscale bargaining point in pricey marriage breakups."

Josie wanted to hit someone. Or something. The very thought of using a child as a bartering chip made her stomach rise up toward her throat. "That's despicable."

"A lot of folks think that fathers or the whole two-parent idea is overrated, and they'll cite successful single parents to make their case. But if true, to deliberately lie to an agency with a marriage requirement for this particular adoption is fraud. We just don't know for sure that's what they did."

"How expensive is the inquiry?" She hated

to ask, and she'd pay whatever was required, but it wasn't like she was made of money. Far from it.

"Pro bono," he told her.

She scoffed. "Cruz, I can pay my own way. I have to. This is my deal, not yours, and don't think you can slip this woman money behind my back and take care of things. I can handle this."

"Good to know, but I mean it," he told her. "Cait had me organize her parents' retirement funds last year, and I was able to get them out of a serious logjam of events before their funds tumbled into nothingness. She's happy to return the favor now. No cost, Josie. Although if you make me barbecue now and again, I'll consider that my tip."

No cost. She'd been fully prepared to hand over a large chunk of her resettlement money from Carrington. Now she wouldn't have to. "And you'll call me as soon as she knows anything?"

"Yes. Or I'll stop by and see you." He indicated The Square, the upscale shopping and gathering spot in the town's center, with a glance toward the window. "This town hears everything, even with windows closed and doors locked."

Josie knew the truth in that, another reason

she'd kept her silence. She'd embarrassed her family by being the talk of the town once. She'd done her best to avoid it since. "Like any small town, I suppose." She stood up and shook his hand. "Thank you, Cruz. And remember—"

"My lips are sealed." He tapped the Carrington contract. "Let me tweak this and I'll send it on to them and you for approval. Oh, and Josie?"

He was going to tell her this was a stupid idea, to accept the Carrington offer and work right there, with Jacob and Addie close by. And he'd be right. She knew that.

Cruz said nothing of the kind. He reached out and took her hands in his. "This is a gutsy move on your part."

Gutsy or foolish? She waited for him to continue.

"And I want to tell you that any mother who can do what you've done, to put the best interests of her child first, both when you gave her up and when you risked your life to save hers…" He gripped her hands. "That ranks you pretty high up on my list. Sacrificial love is a wonderful thing."

The praise came from the lips of a man who'd had an egocentric mother. If anyone appreciated good parenting, it was Cruz Maldonado. "Thank you, Cruz."

"I'll be in touch."

She walked back to her car in the municipal lot, conflicted.

She didn't want to risk having Addie in the middle of grown-up drama. But how else was she to ascertain the O'Neills' history, and Addie's placement with Jacob? What could go wrong besides absolutely everything?

If Jacob discovered her true identity, what would stop him from leaving with Addie? A talented man who'd overseen major projects could work anywhere. He could leave at a moment's notice, and then where would she be?

But she couldn't stand by, inactive. She couldn't assume things were all right for Addie, when so much had gone wrong in her early life. If nothing else, she needed the truth. Yes, she'd stayed silent of her own volition. She'd had her reasons, and she'd trusted the systems in place.

If what she suspected was true, the systems hadn't let her down. Two lying, scheming adults, putting their own agendas first, had done that. A slow burn started somewhere along her midspine and rose upward.

Nobody was allowed to mess with the sweet sanctity of a child for selfish desires. Not on her watch. And while Ginger O'Neill had seemed devoted to Addie, if she'd begun the process based on a lie, then she'd voided at least the moral part of the contract. And that was enough to thrust Josie forward.

"You're here. Good." Jacob rose from his desk in the work trailer as Josie came up the metal steps the next afternoon. He crossed the narrow space and opened the door. "I've just printed up the signature copies of the amended agreement. Carrington agreed on all points except one."

"A deal breaker?" She lifted her right brow and gave him the same look his daughter offered on a regular basis. Part scoffing, part teasing.

"I hope not. They want a long-term contract. They want to know they've got you on board for at least five years. They'd prefer ten for longevity's sake, but I talked them down to five. The two-year option your lawyer cited is off the table because if you walk after two years, we lose a whole lot of work and momentum. Are you all right with that?"

"Five it is."

"Good." He handed her the pen, relieved. He'd been surprised to see the twenty-four month amendment, and not surprised when Carrington officials balked. No new enterprise wanted to risk a major schedule upset two years in. She bent to sign the contract. When she did, her long rust-brown hair tumbled over her shoulder, obscuring her face from his angle.

The warm smell of cinnamon wafted to him. And nutmeg? Maybe. With something else, a pungent, woodsy scent. She smelled of fall in the spring, and why did he find that singularly attractive?

She finished signing and flipped her hair back over her shoulder as she straightened.

The scent hit him again, hints of warm spices on a vibrant May afternoon. And for some reason, on her, it fit. "Is it all right if I send a crew over first thing in the morning to gather the equipment and supplies?"

"Tomorrow is fine. And if it makes things easier, I can have all of my stuff out of the restaurant and apartment by Friday."

Easier? The delay caused by her argument over eminent domain had pushed the lakeshore part of the project into crisis mode. A lakeside hotel with no docking facilities wasn't conducive to a successful grand opening. "You don't need the full thirty days?"

"Not if your crew is doing the big stuff. I travel light."

"We'd appreciate it, Josie."

"All right." She tucked her purse strap a little farther up her shoulder. "I'll head out. Is Addie at school?"

"For the next four weeks. Followed by summer vacation and a two-week spot with no child care."

"How does that happen?"

He made a face. "I didn't realize that the school calendar up north differed from the South. I assumed, and it got me into trouble."

"What will you do with Addie?"

He shrugged. "I'm not sure yet. It's the worst possible timing. I even checked with your cousin, the one who runs the other preschool everyone talks about."

"Rory."

"Yes, but she's closed for those two weeks, too."

"It's kind of a thing here, for the schools to close down and reopen after the Independence Day weekend. I didn't realize that was unique."

"I suppose every area has their scheduling quirks."

"Climate and agriculturally inspired. Or folks just need a little time to regroup. If you need help, let me know."

Let her know?

"We've got several nice college kids who come back in May to work summer jobs," she explained. "A lot of them might be spoken for already, but it's a possibility. Or I could watch her. I'm going to be staying in my aunt's apartment over her garage. It's right in the village, just behind The Square. There would be kids in and out all the time, the whole Gallagher crew. And I'm not working until you have a kitchen in place over here, so it could work. Just a thought."

"I'll think about it, sure." He wouldn't think about it. He didn't know her. He didn't know the college kids she talked about, either.

Did you know the teacher at the day school before you signed Addie up? No.

That was different. It was a registered school.

His internal voice sighed. Because of course nothing bad could ever happen at a registered school.

"I expect you're busy now, but I'd like to go over the kitchen layout before everything's put in place. Placement of the gas lines is pretty clutch in an operation like mine."

"I'll have the kitchen designer set up a time with you."

"Perfect." She didn't push about Addie.

Good.

The thought of leaving Addie with anyone bothered him, which meant he needed to look into a nanny wherever they decided to settle. And that meant a house. A yard. Serious commitments for a man who had been married to his work for a long time.

A firm in Texas had contacted him about overseeing a major project bordering Waco. And a major Arizona development corporation had sent out feelers through their chief operating officer because they were contemplating a three-stage, multiyear all-inclusive adult living community with recreational built-ins.

Carrington was slated to begin a new Outer Banks project. That one would win the choice if his parents hadn't sold their Georgia home and moved to lower Florida. His mother had proclaimed she was ready to be done with winter, but maybe that wasn't the whole story. Maybe being in the town where she'd raised two children and lost one was just too much.

He walked to his car, wondering what his mother would think of the long, cold winter he'd just experienced here.

She'd hate it, but he hadn't minded it at all. He'd enjoyed it, actually. So had Addie. They'd gone sledding and ice skating together, and he hadn't minded that they held each other up on the ice because that's kind of what they'd been doing all along.

His phone rang.

He'd figure out those two gaping weeks in child care later. Right now there was work to be done, and then he needed to drive to the southeast end of the lake and pick up Addie. If the late-day rain held off, maybe he'd take her for a walk along the public beach at the north end. She'd like that. And as multiple work crews worked long hours to get the Eastern Shore Inn up and running by July 1, he wouldn't mind a short break himself.

"Stan's Frozen Custard doesn't fix everything, but it fixes most things." Kimberly bumped cones with Josie while Drew fed the soft, delicious dessert to their toddler son with a spoon. "So you're moving up in the world, Jo-Jo." She teased with the childhood nickname. "The dive owner is now part of the major resort hotel chain. Who knows? If they like you enough, we can make you a franchise and folks up and down the coast can enjoy Bayou Barbecue all year round."

"What are we talking about?" Drew applied a soft napkin to Davy's cheek before the little fellow could blot chocolate ice cream with a white cotton sleeve.

"The Eastern Shore Inn is letting Josie move the Bayou Barbecue into their first-floor casual restaurant area, the part overlooking the beach. Isn't that amazing?" Kimberly's enthusiasm didn't match the look Drew shot Josie.

"Amazing, all right. What made you think of that, Josie?" He didn't call her out, but she read the warning in his voice. "Last I knew you were trying to block the sale of your land, and now a few days later, you're consorting with the enemy?" He lifted his eyes again, and she saw when he made the connection. "You think this is a good idea, Josie? Really?"

How could she answer that in front of Kimberly?

You could try telling Kimberly the truth...

There was no one around right then. They were alone, at the water's edge, overlooking the strip of public beach bordering the north end of the lake. A beautiful night, quiet and still, before the busy hum of summer and cottage dwellers grew to a roar. "I—"

"Hey! Miss Josie! Hey there!"

Josie swallowed the words when a sweet Southern voice hailed her. She made a quarter turn, and there was Addie, racing up the beach, copper curls flying as she kicked up sand. Jacob followed behind her at a more leisurely pace. "It's hard to run in sand! Did you know that?"

"Best training there is for distance runners. How are you?"

"I am so good! My dad promised me we'd walk along the beach and then get ice cream, and I think that's like the best two things of all, don't you?"

Drew had finished wiping Davy down. He stood. Kimberly was looking at Addie, delighted with the girl's enthusiasm, while Drew gazed at Josie.

A part of her hated that he knew, but when she read his look of understanding, she tried to calm her racing heart.

"Hey, Dad, do you care if I sign up for the advanced babysitting course with Callan and Tee for next weekend?" Drew's daughter Amy had crossed over from the Gallagher side of the street. "It's an all-day Saturday thing, and I'd kind of like to get it done before my baseball schedule goes into full swing."

Amy had made the cut for the hardball team when she first arrived in town and had been playing with the boys ever since.

Drew looked at Kimberly. "Are you expecting to have that baby before Saturday?"

"I can't think of anything that would make me happier," she told him, and winked at Amy. "If I'm not here to help with the running around, Josie's got some time off. Do you mind, Jo-Jo?"

"Not at all."

"Jo-Jo?" Addie giggled out loud. "That's like such a fun name, isn't it?"

"For little kids and sassy cousins, yes." Jacob drew closer. She'd bent to reply to Addie.

Now she straightened. "Perfect night for a walk along the beach," Josie said.

"Our first since the weather broke," said Jacob. "I heard this end of the lake is a major gathering spot over the summer."

"With ice cream!" Addie fist-pumped the air.

"Stan's Frozen Custard is the best around," said Kimberly. "You must have just missed last summer's season."

"We came in on the end, but with start-up details and Addie's schooling, it took me a couple of weeks to get acclimated," Jacob replied. "Settling into a new project and a new place can be taxing."

Too taxing to do fun things with a beloved child? Irritation snaked its way up Josie's spine. "I'm sure it is."

Drew shot her a quick look of warning. She pretended not to notice as she asked the next question. "Have you decided on a project when this one's done?"

Jacob shook his head. "There are offers on the table. Nothing that's jumping out at me at the moment. Once Addie's done with school, I'll get serious about locking something in. My daughter's not a fan of hot, humid stretches, and while I've got a couple of good options in the Southwest, I think she'd be miserable down there." He palmed her head with his already suntanned hand, and when she tipped a smile up to him, the effect was pure joy. "She must be carrying northern blood in her veins because once we got here, she took to Grace Haven like a duck takes to water."

Breath escaped Josie.

She tried to will her heart to slow down, but it refused to listen.

Did Jacob mean that? Was he sending out feelers? Or was he simply making a fatherly comment about a cute kid?

"I don't like things really hot, unless maybe it's for a little while," Addie announced to the entire group. "And I loved going sledding with my dad. It was like the best ever!" She raised a finger and pretended to underline the last three words for emphasis. "And he really, really, really liked taking me."

"I've never been quite that cold or that happy in my life," Jacob admitted, and the way he said it put Josie's heart back in a sinus rhythm.

He loved Addie.

The sweet emotion was there in everything he said or did. Did that make her the bad guy in all of this?

How could it, when she was the one led astray? But then she remembered her driver's education instructor, drilling into their heads that the person with the last possible chance to stop an accident from happening bears as much guilt as the person who moves in error.

If you can stop, do it. Always be willing to apply the brakes.

That's what Mr. Bronkowski used to say as he lectured about reducing speed to save lives, and his common-sense directives had stayed with her all these years.

Was she making trouble? Or fixing trouble? Seeing Addie grin up at her adoptive uncle/father, Josie wasn't quite as sure as she'd been a few hours before.

Chapter Five

I will not cry.

Regret mixed with apprehension as Josie watched the skilled team of men package and roll her cache of kitchen equipment into clean, white panel trucks. They handled things with care, and the man and woman assigned to pre-package the smaller kitchen essentials treated her scuffed-up corn bread pans with as much tenderness as they did her stoneware ramekins for crème brûlée, a Bayou mainstay on the dessert menu.

It wasn't the move she was regretting. The choice to stay had been taken out of her hands.

But maybe she was being foolish on multiple levels. Would she be subject to the whims of hotel executives by renting their space? Would they know better than to boss the kitchen boss? And more important, had she traded her hard-won autonomy for a chance to mess up two lives?

"I can't believe they work this quickly."

The rolling whir of metallic dollies had screened Jacob's car. His voice took her by surprise. He apologized quickly, which only made him seem nicer. "Didn't mean to startle you. I just wanted to make sure things were going all right, and Dale had texted me that the smoker might have to come in pieces."

Her smoker was a brute of an outdoor apparatus. She should have built the massive device on a trailer, but didn't because she never imagined moving it. "It's custom-made. And huge. And ridiculously heavy."

He followed her to the far side of the building and whistled lightly when he caught sight of her pride-and-joy piece of equipment. "Whoa."

"I should have made it mobile, but I wasn't planning on smoking at catered events. And it seemed silly to mount it when I planned on staying here, but as you can see, it's a monster."

She wasn't sure what she expected as Jacob inspected the oil-tank-size smoker with layered smoking racks inside, but when he snapped several pictures from multiple angles, she had to ask. "Are you taking pictures to show the insurance company when we make a claim after we try to move it?"

"Not going to move it."

"No?"

He shook his head.

"But that's a cornerstone of Bayou beef, pork and chicken," she told him. "Knowing what to smoke, how to season, spacing, crowding, layering. My smoker is an integral part of how I do business, Jacob."

"If it's been created once, it can be created again, right?"

She supposed so, but who would—

"I think it's more cost-effective if we rebuild on-site, and to avoid this problem ever again, we'll use a heavy-duty trailer base. I'd also like to commission a smaller version for catering. Even if we're not really smoking per se at the event, people like the effect of having the smoker on hand."

"You look that far ahead? Even though your part in all this will be over by then?" His oversight would be complete in a few months. He'd mentioned that last evening.

Her question surprised him. "Because it's the right way to do things, isn't it? To plan this out with an eye toward the future? My dad always taught me to look ahead, plan big and dream bigger." He shrugged. "If we're going full tilt toward making the Bayou Barbecue part of the inn, knowing folks will love that you're still right here on the lake, why not go at it with a workable plan? You've done catering here." He indicated the two decorated vans parked on the backside of the lot. "Why should this year be any different?"

Clearly he was missing the importance of a timeline when it came to restaurant food. "Because we're going to be closed for six weeks? Because it's hard to schedule parties when your business is in limbo? I was tied up in litigation until this week," she reminded him. "I didn't take on anything, I refused all requests because I had no idea if I'd even be in business this summer, Jacob."

He ran a hand across his chin and winced slightly. "I hadn't considered that fully. This move isn't just affecting a six-week window, it's affected an entire season. But we can start booking for the late summer and fall season, can't we? And if Carrington makes the announcement that you're coming on board, and advertises accordingly…"

"And books a spot at the annual Christkindl and the Lumberjack Festival over in Macedon, plus any other festivals planned from Independence Day on—"

"That's a great idea." He tapped a message into his phone, then hit Send. "I'm going to have my assistant see what food vendor spaces might still be available at local festivals, and Carrington will cover the entry fees to lock in the space. If we can make up for some of the lost time by being a visible presence locally, that will help maintain the local clientele and get folks used to seeing you or whoever is running the catering truck out and about. Unfortunately, we're hitting your name recognition at the worst possible time." He looked upset by that for just a moment, but then he snapped his fingers and hooked his thumb toward the nearly finished inn up the beach. "Why do we have to wait?"

"Because I have no kitchen?" She pointed toward the second truck that had just pulled away, moving the guts of her endeavor into storage.

"What if we create a pseudo kitchen in the interim?" he asked. "If we can get enough equipment up and running to service the takeout shack, then we could keep business going, folks would still be able to get barbecue the first weeks of summer, and how hard can it be to have loaded cowboy baked potatoes and shaved beef or pork sandwiches? If we focus on simple, it could work, right?"

Her head spun, and not just because he was tossing out possibilities to help her while she was ingratiating herself to turn his life upside down. And how did a land developer know anything about running a restaurant? "How do you know all this? The average guy off the street doesn't know how to run a dive-type experience that's really a first-class operation in casual disguise. And yet..." She paused, gazing at him, and for just a moment, she wanted to keep on gazing at him. His eyes, kind and strong. His voice, commanding but helpful. And don't get her started on the broad set of his shoulders in today's more casual attire.

She gave herself a mental wake-up call. Wasn't she already on shaky ground? No reason to mess things up further. "You seem to have a handle on it."

"I leave the hotel incidentals up to the experts who run hotels, but when we incorporate a restaurant, the best thing to do is get it up off the ground as soon as possible. You've already done that, but if we can keep momentum going, in a casual manner, then we don't lose time rebuilding business. And time is money. My dad ran a chain of chicken places down south," he added, smiling. "I've been restaurant savvy from the time I could walk. He taught me the basics of development, site prep and running a business from beginning to end."

"Does he still run the restaurants?"

Jacob's expression went quiet. He stared off, over her shoulder, toward the water.

"No. He retired a couple of years ago. He'd made a fortune, and my mother had planned a big party to celebrate moving on, having some time together, but then…my sister was killed in a horrible accident. It took the heart out of them. They canceled the party, completed the sale on the businesses and moved to southern Florida on the Gulf side. My father hates it, my mother pretends to love it, and neither one has gotten over their grief."

Broken hearts littered his family, just like hers. Did that affect things, though? Did their loss negate Ginger's deception, if that's what happened six years ago?

"I pray for them every day," he went on. "They're such good people. They've worked so hard and done a lot of good in their time, but there's an emptiness they can't fill no matter what they do." He sent her a look of regret. "I keep hoping they'll find peace or happiness somehow. Or somewhere. They can't seem to get over being mad, and I think that happens sometimes when you've got lots of money." He faced her more directly. "You don't expect things to go wrong, because money fixes everything. Except when it doesn't."

Sage words from a person of faith.

But she couldn't let herself get off track. She could accept that Jacob was a good man and still investigate what happened when Ginger and Adam O'Neill signed those adoption papers. Her beef wasn't with the kind, handsome man standing alongside her. It was with two people who were now out of the picture.

But she couldn't kid herself.

Ginger and Adam wouldn't be hurt by whatever happened here. Jacob would. That couldn't be helped, but knowing that didn't make her happy. Not in the least.

Josie Gallagher was easy to talk to. Maybe too easy, Jacob realized on the drive back to the inn, because Jacob wasn't a talker by nature. But when she stood there, her expression intent, he knew she wasn't just listening politely. She was hearing him, and the understanding in her eyes loosened his tongue even more.

But as receptive as she was, he couldn't forget that he'd be leaving in a couple of months, and she'd be here, running her highly regarded restaurant in a new location. He wanted it to work out for her, and he'd been pleased when she accepted the offer to come on board with the inn.

But she'd surprised him, too.

After balking so firmly, to have her quietly acquiesce seemed out of character.

Out of character? Like you know her that well?

Maybe out of sync with their initial meeting was a better assessment, he decided. He didn't know her well, but he knew enough to realize he liked what he saw. She was unique, and not just in womanly ways. Josie Gallagher marched to her own drummer, and while he couldn't deny he found that attractive, she'd need to fall in line somewhat to make the transition from freestanding restaurant to being part of an enclave. Judging from what he'd seen so far, Josie didn't worry all that much about blending.

He pulled into the service parking area on the backside of the hotel. One moving van had already pulled in there. The others had taken the bulk of Josie's equipment to the massive trailer parked between his office trailer and the hotel. The crew would store her stuff there while the kitchen was made ready. He'd set up a meeting with Josie and Maybelle, the kitchen designer Carrington had brought on board, and when Josie's small car pulled in forty-five minutes later, he pretended he hadn't been watching for it.

She didn't cross the hard hat area this time, but that might be because she saw him watching. She paused, swept the work area a slow, searching gaze, then grinned and stayed to the right side of the tape barriers. She didn't duck under to purposely tweak him and the crew, but she acted like she wanted to, and for some reason, that made him feel lighter inside. "You resisted temptation," he said as she strolled up the walk. She darted a glance behind him, and her eyes lit up.

"Only because I didn't want to get you riled up before our meeting with the kitchen queen."

"Kitchen queen?" He halted as Maybelle approached from the opposite direction. "Um…"

"You got that right." The dark-skinned woman grinned as she drew closer. "When I heard that you were steppin' in on the ground floor, I said to myself, now there's a Yankee with just enough sass and sauce to be Cajun to the core. How are you doin', Josie June?"

"Delighted to be working with the best of the best," Josie told her, then hugged the stout older woman. "I couldn't believe it when I saw you walking this way, but there's only one Maybelle Watts who runs the kitchen circuit, and here you are."

"You two know each other?" Jacob looked from one to the other. "How is that possible?"

"I worked in Louisiana bayou country for several years," Josie told him. "And Maybelle had done the design on two of the biggest and best Cajun kitchens cable TV can offer. I borrowed all the ideas I used in my place from things she'd already set up for Big Bobby and Tuck. Maybelle, it's a pleasure and an honor to be working with you."

"Well, let's get down to it, then. I'm not used to settin' things up and worryin' 'bout winter for six months of the year, so this is something of a challenge," Maybelle said as they moved into the soon-to-be-finished hotel. "But the space they've allotted is sweet, and if we can have a covered area back here—" she waved toward the back access door "—where the smoker can be set up for year-round use, but folks don't have to be standing hip deep in snow to take care of things? That would be good."

Jacob was busily making notes in his small, electronic tablet when Maybelle added, "And I'm talkin' to Tuck tonight, as a matter of fact! My youngest ended up marryin' his son and they're due to have a baby soon, so Tuck and I wanted to throw a little Cajun-style shower for them. Wait till I tell him I ran into you, Josie! He'll be pleased as punch that you're doin' so well."

Maybelle kept walking, but Josie stopped. So did Jacob, watching her.

She put a hand to her throat, teasing the gold

chain she wore bearing one small medallion of some sort. "He probably won't even remember me, Maybelle. I'd just leave it alone."

"Not remember you?" Maybelle dismissed that quickly. "He told me that the stupidest thing he did was let Big Bobby tempt you away, and he won't be a bit surprised that you've done well up here. He always knew you would."

They'd talked about her.

And if Maybelle meant what she said, they'd be talking again tonight. Except that Tuck was one of the few people who knew about Addie. Oh, he didn't know details, but he knew she'd gotten pregnant…and how…and knew she'd signed away her rights. He'd been a father figure to her in the midst of crazy, and what if he said anything to Maybelle when they talked?

"Are you all right?"

She wasn't one bit all right, but she had to pretend…and then go on pretending. "Yes." She moved forward, but not with the ease she'd felt moments before.

What were the odds that Carrington would hire the one kitchen designer with a direct line to her past? And why didn't she consider that a Southern-based company would pull in the best design people from the Southern circuit?

They talked methods, habits and placement, crew access, cooler needs and wood-fired ovens. And when they were done, Maybelle slipped her little notebook into a generous-size purse and called the meeting over. "I've got what I need," she declared. She patted the large leather bag. "I'm going back to the temporary office up the road to put this together with my software. Jacob." She turned to him. "I'll have plans to you by noon tomorrow. I know we need to get on top of this, so I'll include an equipment list for anything we don't have documented from Josie's kitchen. In the meantime, if you get the crew on developing the covered smoker area outside the west bay, you should be able to jump on the idea for your take-out shack within a week. Hook up the roasting oven, the portable catering warmers, the slicer and the bun warmer."

He typed quickly as she spoke.

"Anything else, Josie?"

"If we've got a smoker, we can do ribs," she added. "My slathering sauce can be made off-site and put in the warmers."

"Adding ribs." He typed that into his electronic notebook. "If you think of anything else, Maybelle, text me. Or email it. Whatever works for you. And I'll have the foreman assign a crew to create the covered area out here."

"No flat roof," Josie warned him. "If we get a bad winter, a flat roof on this side of the building is going to pile up snow. Prevailing winds will transform the hotel into a pricey snow fence, and the snow will dump in drifts right here." She pointed to the present configuration of roofline and lake.

"I wouldn't have thought of that." Jacob made another note. "Thanks, Josie. That could've been a costly mistake."

"I'm out." Maybelle patted Jacob's shoulder, but she reached out and hugged Josie. "It is a pleasure to see you doing so well, and I can't wait to tell Tuck. He'll be so pleased!"

She'd have to call her old boss and warn him off. Ask him to stay quiet.

She knew Tuck, he had a good heart, but he liked to talk, and when it came to things like this, talk was dangerous.

Worry didn't snake up her spine. It leaped, with cat feet. She clenched her shoulders, then her neck and the ensuing headache was a warning that she needed to relax, but how could she?

She'd started something. She had to see it through, but when a small bus pulled up to the loop and dropped Addie off just then, the far-reaching consequences of her choices hit her anew.

Did she have the right to mess up Addie's life, if all was well and good with Jacob?

"I'm home!" Addie raced across the sidewalk as the bus driver gave a friendly wave. "And have I got papers for you, Dad! Like the best ones ever, and Miss Gilly says I might be the brightest little poppet she's ever had the privilege to know!"

"She said that, huh?" He bent, grinning. "Gosh, I love how you talk, kid."

"Well, that was what she said," she explained in her adorable, take-charge voice. "But I'm glad you love it, anyway." She handed him the papers, then did something that made Josie's fears dance anew even as it strengthened her resolve.

Addie hugged her.

The spontaneous embrace felt so right. So very right. And even if it was wrong, it didn't feel that way, so she hugged the little girl back.

Oh, her heart.

To hug her daughter, her precious child, her little girl after all this time.

She'd never imagined this opportunity. She'd thought about what she'd do if Addie ever came looking for her. Would she understand the choices Josie made? Or would she feel abandoned? Cast off?

She'd wondered that often, but right now, none of it mattered because she was holding her little girl. If science claimed a heart couldn't physiologically grow, it was wrong. Dead wrong. Because her heart grew in that moment. And when Addie released her, Josie knew neither she—nor her heart—would ever be the same again.

Her phone beeped a message, and Josie used it for an escape route. "Gotta run. Jacob, thank you for all of your help. I'm going to head up the beach and get the rest of my stuff ready to move into my aunt's apartment in town. Things will be easier here if I'm settled there."

"You'll get to live right near the ice-cream store?" Addie didn't try to mask the delight in her voice or expression.

"A short walk away, and an even greater temptation," Josie assured her. "Stan's custard is a town favorite. That's why I brought them on board at the Bayou. It made sense to help another local business, and gave people a proximity to the best custard around without having to drive twenty minutes north and hunt for parking."

"That's the same business mentality that brought you into the inn," Jacob noted. "My dad calls it the restaurant overview, and not too many have it."

Josie hadn't thought of it that way, but he was right. And wrong. Because a big reason for her accepting the deal was standing less than two feet away. "Great minds think alike."

"See you later, Josie! I love your hair!"

"I feel the exact same about yours, sweet thing."

Addie preened, then slung her pink-and-silver backpack over her shoulder.

Josie walked back to her car, reweighing her choices.

Addie was delightful and self-assured for a reason. She didn't have a clue about any early life shenanigans that might have occurred. She knew love. She'd been carried to term, given to a woman who clearly loved her, and was now with a man who doted on her.

Josie had no right to upset that. And yet...

How could she gloss over the original deceit that brought them all here? It didn't sit right with her.

She climbed into her car, but when she got out onto the road, she didn't go straight back to her apartment.

She needed help. She needed advice. And she needed it from people who should have known what was going on long ago. She hit the Bluetooth and made three calls: to Kimberly, to her aunt Kate and then the hardest call of all—her mother.

Cissy Gallagher thought she knew her daughter. She was about to find out that wasn't the case, and Josie didn't have a clue how to ease into any of that.

Chapter Six

Jacob took the call from his father while Addie ran a stream of small cars along tiny roads she'd made in the sand. "Dad, hey. How's it going?"

"It's all right," Bob Weatherly told him. "But already unseasonably hot, and your mother's been craving some grandkid time, so we're going to head your way next week and stay a while. We booked a cottage across the lake from where you're building. I haven't seen your mother this excited for a while. It's positively refreshing."

"She wants to see Addie."

"And you. But yes, she hasn't seen Addie since Christmas, and she misses her. How is everything? Is the hotel construction on schedule? Is everything working out all right?"

"It is. You miss working. I can tell."

"More than I can say," his dad admitted. "I

don't know what I was thinking, especially so soon after losing Ginger. Having her gone magnified everything, and then leaving Georgia, leaving you, coming down here. I keep thinking I should have a do-over, but life doesn't come with those, does it?"

"Sure it does." Jacob kept his voice casual on purpose. "With faith."

"Well, it's a comfort to some, I know."

How hard should he press?

Not hard at all, Jacob decided. He'd lead by example, and simple words. Bob Weatherly wasn't the kind to be pushed into anything. Jacob liked to think he was similar, only not quite as stubborn. "It is. When are you getting in?"

"We've got the place for two weeks, and if we want to stay longer, we'll either rebook or find another spot."

"There's not really a lot available after Memorial Day, I've been told."

"There's always something available for the right price, son."

In his father's world that was more true than not. "Addie will be thrilled to see you guys, but go easy on the presents, okay? I'm not sure what our plans are right now, and having an extra ten crates to move won't be fun."

"You'll come south, of course."

The minute Bob said it, Jacob decided to stay north, and he recognized the knee-jerk reaction right away. "Haven't decided anything, yet, but the job offers are coming in. I figured I'd sort things out once we get closer to grand opening."

"We can talk while we're there, then."

"Sure, Dad." He heard his mother's voice in the background. "Give Mom my love, won't you?"

"I sure will. And you tell that granddaughter of mine I can't wait to see her!"

"Will do." He hung up the phone, torn. Not because they were coming to visit. He was glad they were showing a spark of their old selves, when grabbing hold of life and doing things had been seamless.

But he'd noticed something at Christmas. His father didn't do idle well. Golfing, traveling, hanging out and playing cards were fine for some, and his mother didn't mind the change. But his father had second-guessed everything Jacob said or did at Christmas, and he did it because he was accustomed to running the show.

Addie raced his way.

He put away the phone and grinned at the sight. The bright coppery hair, topped by a saucy cap, the sailor shirt and capris, the lime-green beach shoes.

She was a page from a catalog, and anyone seeing her would gladly plunk down money for the whole package, she was that endearing.

He couldn't let his parents spoil her. He'd seen the tendency at Christmas, and he'd stayed quiet because loss hit hard at Christmas. Holidays and grief made a sorry mix.

But Ginger had been gone over two years now. Addie had adjusted well. She didn't like not having a mom, and she made that clear, but she didn't ask about Ginger anymore, either. Losing a parent at such a young age was both bane and blessing. At age four, a child didn't understand the permanency of death, and after a while, she'd just stopped asking.

The sad part was that she might not ever have real, firm memories of her mother, and that was harsh. But on the positive side she remembered being loved. That was the best blessing of all. "How about supper?"

"I was hoping for fish and chips?"

He laughed because what six-year-old hoped for fish and chips?

His.

"Let's do it. And then a bath before bed because you can't go off to school tomorrow with today's sand in your hair."

"Okay!"

She took his hand. She'd done that at her

mother's funeral, as others walked away, heads bowed.

She'd watched them settle flowers on her mother's casket, with no real idea what it all meant, and then she'd reached up and clasped his hand. And she didn't let go. And that's how it had been ever since. "I like that Miss Josie's coming to work with us."

"She's not." He spoke instantly, then wondered why.

"She is so, silly!" Addie brought to task, laughing. "Her restaurant is going to be in our hotel, right?"

"Except it's not ours," he reminded her. "I'm only working on it."

"Well, it's like ours, for now," she conceded. "And I'm still happy that Miss Josie's going to be there with us. I think she makes the best French toast ever, and she thinks my hair is pretty."

"Reason enough to love her, right there." He settled a dry look on his romance-loving daughter. "Do not try and set me up with Josie or anyone else, okay? I can find my own dates."

"Then how come you never do?" She sent him a look of frank appraisal as she fastened her belt. "Dad, it's not that hard. You ask a lady out, you dance and you fall in love. It happens all the time on TV."

"I suppose that's true." But life didn't copy television. Not generally. "Let things happen as they will, okay? Don't force God's hand. And for a quick change of subject, Pawpaw and Memaw are coming to visit next week. They want to see you, and school's almost over, so they're going to hang out and visit."

"I can't believe this!" Addie slapped a hand to her forehead. "I was just thinking that I wanted to see Memaw and Pawpaw, and this happens! Oh that will be so wonderful, won't it Dad?"

"It sure will." He wanted it to be fun, and he was pretty sure it would be, on her end. But if his father pushed like he had at Christmas, criticizing everything Jacob did, then they'd have to have a frank discussion, and Jacob knew his father well. He didn't like being called out. Maybe…just maybe…something would come along to keep his father's brain engaged and let Jacob off the hook but for the life of him, Jacob couldn't imagine what that might be.

Cissy Gallagher crossed the room and knelt in front of Josie. She grasped one of Josie's hands while Kimberly thrust tissues at both of them. "You have a daughter?"

"Yes."

"Oh, baby." By the time mother and daughter

were able to speak coherently, half a box of tissues had disappeared. "Why didn't you tell me? I would have helped you. You're my daughter, my child, Josie. I'd do anything for you."

"I'd messed up so badly before, and you begged me not to go."

"But that was years before this happened. Didn't you think all that time being straight and true would have regained my trust?"

Josie shrugged. "I can't say I was thinking all that clearly, except on one detail. I wanted my daughter to have the best chance possible to have a full, normal life as someone's cherished child. And with the circumstances of her conception, I would either be living a lie or telling a child the heinous truth no child should hear. Plus——" she paused, took a deep breath and faced her mother "——I didn't think anyone would believe me. You guys knew how badly I'd messed up at Fredonia. I'd betrayed your trust then, and got the whole town talking about the wild Gallagher girl. I didn't want any of that to sift down to Addie."

"So what's changed?" Cissy asked. "Because I can see in your face that something's gone terribly wrong."

Josie explained what had happened earlier that week. "I've got Drew looking into Jacob Weatherly's history, and Cruz has a friend who specializes in adoptions. She's looking into the original transfer from me to the O'Neills. I think they lied on their application," she explained. "I don't think they ever intended to stay together, and my request of this agency, a request the agency honored, was to have my daughter placed with a happily married couple. They had to sign an affidavit to that effect. I've got nothing against single-parent families," she added. "But with such a big decision in front of me, I wanted the odds in the baby's favor. Now it appears Addie's adoptive father was out of the picture within days of the finalized adoption. As if he couldn't wait to get out and move on."

Kate put one hand over Josie's. "That could make the original adoption null and void, couldn't it?" When Josie grimaced, Kate patted her hand. "And now you're caught in the middle. You gave her life, you then went and saved her life, the most wonderful act any mother can do, and now here she is, with the wrong person…but she's happy, so how do you upset an apple cart that seems to be successfully carting around piles of apples?"

"That's a horrible analogy, Mom. But apt." Kimberly held up one finger. "First of all, I can't believe you never told me any of this, except that I honestly get it." When Josie made a doubtful face, Kimberly waved it off. "No,

I do. I was kind of a jerk in Nashville, and there's a history there I'd prefer we leave hidden forever, and the fiancé dumping me before I moved back here was only the tip of that iceberg of stupidity. So I probably understand far more than you know, but here's the thing. It's May. He's going to be here with Addie until after the grand opening July 1, and that leaves you time to digest the facts and then decide what to do. Can you talk to him about this? Like face-to-face, grown-up style?"

Could she? Josie hesitated. "I think I could, eventually. If I do it now, he's going to think I took the restaurant deal because of Addie."

"Well…" Kimberly's frank expression called her out on that.

"Okay, I did, but I'd have taken it anyway, once I calmed down and got over the fact that big business can just swoop in and kick the little people aside. So maybe in a week or two?"

"He'll know you better. You'll know him better. You said he's single?" Kate asked.

"I only know that because Addie tried to get him to ask me out when we first met."

"Solves everything from my vantage point," said Kate, and when Josie shot her a dark look, Kate ticked off her fingers. "You get a nice guy with a great job, you get your daughter, and a restaurant. Triple win, Josephine June."

Josie leaned closer. "Is this before or after I explain to him that the original adoption decree might be fraudulent and that he might have to give up custody of the child he so clearly loves?"

"When will Cruz know something?"

Josie shook her head. "He was having the adoption attorney go all out, but I don't know how long that might take. It's an awkward situation, and in the end, if I declare myself, I end up doing the very thing I never wanted to do. Mess up my kid with the wretchedness of how she came into this world."

"What does she look like?" Cissy leaned closer, and Kimberly answered before Josie could get a chance.

"You."

"Me?" Cissy lifted both brows. "I had three children, and not one of them resembled me at all. All three look like their dad, God rest his soul, although Josie got a little of my red in her hair color."

"This one has it," Josie told her. "She's the image of you. Copper hair, deep green eyes, just a few freckles, fair skin and that same oval face. She looks like a Morgan, Mom. Like you and your sisters."

"What is her name?"

"Adeline. He calls her Addie."

"I have to see her. Can I come by, Josie? Sometime when she'll be around? I'd just like to see her for myself."

"Cissy." Kate's voice held caution. "Is that the best idea?"

"Would you do it if the situation were reversed?" Cissy asked, and Kate nodded instantly.

"Absolutely. I'd probably be arrested for stalking. The fact that I'd do it doesn't make it the best idea, though."

"We could all stop by to pick Josie up to go shopping for baby things, and then it doesn't look like a setup."

"Fiendishly clever idea." Kate pounced on Kimberly's words like a cat on a mouse. "Then we can discuss the possibilities while we pick out baby things."

"You won't say anything? Any of you?" Josie scanned the three women. Each one solemnly shook her head. "Then all right. I want you to see her. To see how perfectly amazing and beautiful and wonderful she is."

"How about Saturday? You can go over there to check on kitchen things and we'll stop by to pick you up."

Now that she'd told them, how could she prevent them from seeing Addie in person? "And you'll say nothing?"

"Not a word."

"And no tears?" She aimed a strict look at her mother, and Cissy winced.

"Not until we're in the car. Okay?"

It would have to be, because just telling these three women the truth had relieved the ache of carrying this burden alone. "And then we'll talk in the car. Agreed?"

"Agreed."

"Josie, I'm taking tomorrow off so you and I can pack up your things together," Cissy decided. "Now, I know you're perfectly capable of doing all of this yourself…"

Josie bit her tongue and let her mother speak.

"But I want to help you. I need to help you. And I want to make sure you understand that I will always, always be here for you. All right?"

How silly she'd been to think her mother wouldn't believe her. She saw that now, looking into Cissy's face. "Yes, Mom. Absolutely."

"Good." She grabbed Josie and hugged her long and hard. "I'll see you tomorrow. And Josie?"

"Yes?" Josie had a good three inches on her mother, so she looked down into the very same eyes she'd passed on to her daughter.

"I love you."

"I know." She whispered the words, thick with emotion again. "I know, Mom."

Chapter Seven

Jacob parked his SUV on the apartment side of the old Bayou Barbecue the next morning, two spots down from Josie's beat-up Jeep. The back door of the hatch was open and half-full. Boxes and bags were stuffed into every back-seat nook and cranny. She'd obviously started early and stuck with the job.

The May sun shone brightly on tiny leaves, newly unfurled. The late-day forecast promised rain, but for the moment, warmth prevailed. He got to the door just in time to swing it open as Josie approached from inside the apartment. "Here you go."

"Thanks." She looked surprised to see him, and maybe a little uncomfortable? He hoped not, and was kind of surprised that it would bother him. But it did. "I wasn't expecting to see you."

"I had an hour between conference calls, and I wanted to see if you needed help loading things. Your timeline sounded somewhat ambitious yesterday afternoon, and I didn't want you to feel like you had to hit the ground running. At least, not alone."

She set the bundle of hangers into the passenger seat, then faced him. "My mom's coming over shortly. But thank you."

"I've got an hour and empty hands. I'd like to help, Josie."

She lifted her eyes to his, and then she stood there, holding his gaze, as if she couldn't let go, or maybe because she didn't want to let go. And neither did he.

She broke the connection by forcing herself to turn away. "Then yes, welcome aboard. I didn't think there was this much to move, but I realized this morning that I'm a closet stuffer. I'm actually donating everything you see in the back of the Jeep because it's stuff I'll either never wear or use in my lifetime. Which means there are benefits to being forced out of my comfort zone."

"I've found that, too." He followed her inside, and when she pointed to a stack of blue plastic totes, he lifted two of them. "The more comfortable I am, the less inspired I seem to be, so having multiple projects in various venues helped sharpen my abilities. Although, I'm not against finding a place to put roots down now, with Addie needing to be in elementary school. She deserves a chance to have a home, although I'm not exactly the picket-fence type."

"The very image is frightening, isn't it?"

He laughed because that was about the last thing he expected her to say. "Most women I've known would not agree."

"Well, don't get me wrong." Josie picked up a tote and followed him outside. "I like the idea of having a home someday, just not in a neighborhood where talk runs rampant. I've always thought a log cabin, up in the woods, overlooking the lake would be wonderful. Part of the community, but separate enough to do my own thing."

"Self-provided autonomy."

"Yes. I love people, but I like my privacy, too."

"Did you have a plan about where to put these?" he asked, referring to the totes as they drew close to the parking lot. "Because there isn't an inch of room in your car unless you want them next to the stuff you're donating."

A full-size sedan pulled in right then. It swung around and backed up to the sidewalk. The engine shut down as the trunk popped open. "My mother has perfect timing, it seems."

"Can't argue that." He settled the totes into the trunk, then arranged hers alongside as a small woman with red-gold hair climbed out of the front seat.

"Mom, this is Jacob Weatherly. He's overseeing the establishment of the Bayou at the Eastern Shore Inn. Jacob, this is my mother, Cissy Gallagher."

He put out his hand, and she took it with a quick smile. "How nice to meet you, Jacob. I'm quite excited about the possibility this affords, to have the Bayou be part of the inn. It's a marvelous opportunity for year-round business, and that's always a consideration on the lakeshore. How did you handle your first winter in Grace Haven?"

"Surprisingly well," he told her as they walked back toward the apartment. She looked nothing like Josie. Her coloring, face and body type were completely different, but she spoke with a similar intonation. "I was raised in Georgia, and I've done numerous jobs up and down the coast, but I have to say I found the winter refreshing up here. Clean, brisk and cold." He shrugged. "It suited. And my daughter was enchanted by things like sledding, building snowmen, making maple snow with her teacher in school, and while learning to skate was an epic fail for both of us, I'd be willing to try it again if the chance arises."

"I've always enjoyed the respite of winter," Cissy told him as she picked up a stack of small boxes. "It's a regrouping time for me. When spring hits, I can't wait to jump into projects."

"So many projects, so little time." Josie said the words softly, and her mother laughed out loud.

"My daughter knows me well. I bite off more than I can chew, and beg help as needed."

"But she cooks for all of us when we descend on her to help with whatever the current project is, so no one really minds."

"Did you get your love for cooking from your mother?"

Josie set two smaller plastic totes onto the larger ones in the trunk. "My mom loves to cook, so yes. But my father was the kitchen artist, the mad scientist who worked all day and then made a tremendous mess of the kitchen at night. But his methods taught me to attack recipes and results from alternative directions, so between the two of them, it worked."

"Does your mother love to cook, Jacob?" Cissy asked as she stowed a handful of filled plastic bags in and around bigger items.

"My mother is not exactly 'kitchen-friendly,'" he admitted. "My dad ran a chain of restaurants, and my mother's life was filled with other things. We had a cook. And a maid."

"*Downton Abbey*. Be still my heart." Josie pretended to swoon, and he laughed.

"Not to that level, but yes, it was different from what I know now. And that's all right. I like Addie to know that work is a good thing, that effort's important. She likes to cook with me, although we don't do a lot of that on school nights. On the weekend, though." He closed the full trunk and dusted his hands together. "We've been known to destroy a kitchen in our quest for delicious meals. And cupcakes. I can handle cupcakes, and she loves to put on the frosting—a lot of frosting," he admitted. "I probably should draw a line on it, but I can't. Although I always get stuck with the end-of-project chores."

"The joy of cleanup."

He made a face. "She opts out of that quickly. There's always a doll that needs feeding or a picture to color. She's pretty game to help out in most situations, though, so that's solid behavior for her age. And I only know this because I have every child development book and well-reviewed parenting tome on the planet. The ones in English, that is. When I ended up being a surprise dad, I wanted to do everything I could to not mess things up."

"No, of course not."

Josie's quiet voice offered support and something else. Longing, perhaps? Funny, he'd have thought her to be career-centric, but maybe his assumption was wrong. "She is making it quite clear that she's tired of living in apartments."

"It's tough to find an apartment that takes cows," Josie noted.

"Impossible, it seems." He laughed and she laughed, and her mother lifted an eyebrow in question. "Addie wants a cow, and Josie has kindly offered to take us over to the farm on West Lake Road. Your cousin, you said?"

"Yes. Brian. Addie would love to meet his kids. And see his cows."

"Does this Sunday work? We're free midday, after church, if that's all right." He gave a quick look to his watch. He had a few minutes yet, but just a few before he needed to get back to work. He faced her, with the morning sun deepening the auburn tones in her very pretty hair, and waited.

All right?

Josie didn't have to think twice because she'd do whatever she needed to do to have time with Addie. To take her daughter over to Brian's farm, to show her around, to see her pretty green eyes light up when she spotted a pasture full of cows? "Yes, it does, actually. We're doing some baby shopping with Kimberly on Saturday, so Sunday would be great." She closed the door on her mother's backseat and faced him.

"Is noon all right?"

"Perfect."

And then he gave her heart reason to pause when he asked, "Where shall I pick you up?"

Nowhere.

That's what she should say, she should assure him that it wasn't the least bit necessary, and that she could meet him and Addie at Bryan's farm stand at the lake's southern tip…

But she didn't.

She hesitated for less than a nanosecond and said, "178 Creighton Landing, right behind The Square."

"Perfect. Addie will be crazy-excited." His phone buzzed a timely reminder. "I've got to head back to the inn for the call I'm expecting."

"Well, thanks for stopping. For helping." She wasn't sure what to do with her hands as she spoke. It was kind of him to drive over here. To offer help. And then to set up the farm trip with her, but he was being nice because he didn't realize who she was, and the unfairness of that struck her as he waved goodbye.

"This—" her mother watched him go, then faced Josie straight on "—is beyond awkward."

"I know."

"And Kimberly's right. He's quite good-looking and available."

He was good-looking. And nice. So nice. If the circumstances were different—but they weren't. "And he'll hate me when he finds out who I am."

"He'll be surprised," said Cissy. "Understandably so. *Hate*'s a strong word."

Was it? In this instance? Josie wasn't sure, and until she was, or at least until she had more information to go on, she would keep things to herself. At least for a while.

"Will Memaw and Papaw have time to play with me when they're here?" The promised rain had come and gone, leaving a glorious Saturday in its wake, and Jacob's precocious daughter seemed to have gotten a dose of spring fever. "I want to show them everything around here, because our town is so very beautiful, isn't it, Daddy?"

"Our town? At what point did we adopt Grace Haven, Addie-cakes?" They'd come by the worksite for a two-hour stint of checking in with subcontractors. With the grand opening drawing close, the luxury of a no-work Saturday had disappeared with the advent of nice weather.

"Well, I love it, so why not adopt it?" She faced him frankly. She liked to choose her own outfits, and today she'd layered herself in some sort of wacky ensemble that suited her just fine but messed with his ordered sensibilities. He was pretty sure that's why their relationship worked so well. Her eccentricities loosened him up and made him rethink a couple of decades of firm decision-making. "You liked winter here, didn't you?"

"I did," he admitted. "And I'm surprised that I did, but that's not the point, is it?"

"I think it's part of a point, Dad."

He almost laughed out loud, but caught himself because she was being utterly sincere and quite rational. "I need to work, honey. And usually I go where the work calls me."

"But what if you can work in this town?" she insisted. She perched those hands on her hips and squared up. "Dad, I think there are lots of things to do here, and if we love it so much, and it has cows, why should we leave? Have you looked for a job here?" she wondered, head tilted and her cute little eyebrows drawn up.

"Unfortunately, finishing a megamillion-dollar project has kept me tied up, but I promise I'll check things out soon."

"For real?"

She didn't give up easy, that's for sure. "I'll include it in my list of possibilities. I promise," he added when she looked doubtful. He spotted Josie's car pulling into the parking lot near the kitchen area. "Josie just pulled in. Let's walk over and see what's up and we can explain about tomorrow."

Addie had come home from school on Friday night with an impromptu invitation to a Sunday afternoon birthday party for a classmate. Addie's invitation had gotten lost, and when the mother discovered that, she'd emailed Jacob to resend the invite. And, of course, Addie wanted to go, but she longed to visit the farm, too.

Josie spotted them and waved as they approached. "Hey, guys. Beautiful morning, isn't it?"

"The plants got a drink of rain," Addie told her as she hop-skipped up the walk. "It was just like God planned it all out—the warm sun, the drink of rain and now warm sun again. Did you know that plants and animals all need water? Without water we'd shrivel right up." She pretended to do just that, curling inward and making a ghastly dying noise. "And die."

"Then bring on the rain." Josie laughed. "I take it you've been studying the water cycle in school?"

"That is exactly what we're studying, and how did you know that?" Addie half squealed the question in amazement. "Do you know about the water cycle?"

Josie handed over four slim books, banded together. "For you, kid. I had them in my car for tomorrow, but since I'm seeing you today, here you go."

"The Magic School Bus!" Addie slapped a hand to her forehead. "How did you know that I love *The Magic School Bus* show so much?"

"Well, I loved these books when I was your age, so I thought they might be just right for you. I've got more, too. My mom has a whole crate of them. And speaking of my mom, there she is." Josie waved toward a car that seemed to be creeping into the cordoned-off lot, unsure where to go. The driver spotted her and parked. Three women exited the car and came their way. "Jacob, you met my mom and Kimberly over at my place. This is Kimberly's mother, Kate Gallagher, the gal who made Kate & Company one of the biggest and best event co-ordinating centers in the Finger Lakes."

Jacob had heard Kate Gallagher's name before, essentially being synonymous with her highly regarded business. He extended his hand. "You've met with our incoming management team, Mrs. Gallagher, but I haven't had the pleasure as yet. It's very nice to meet you. I hope the inn will become one of your most sought-after business partners."

"We've got seven events lined up so far," she told him, "including four weddings, a Christmas charity gala and two bridal showers. If those go well, I expect Kimberly and the crew will enjoy a long and happy relationship with the Eastern Shore Inn. Your setup is gorgeous, and the positioning on the hill overlooking the lake is perfect for pictures. I can't wait to see it all once the landscaping is in place."

"It'll only get better," he told her, then he turned toward Josie. "We have a scheduling problem for tomorrow." He palmed Addie's head as she made an undeniably cute frowny face toward Josie. "Addie's been invited to a birthday party for a classmate. The invite got lost, and the mom called last night, apologizing. Addie really wants to go to the farm, but she wants to go to the party, too. Can we do the farm another day?"

Josie looked about to answer when her cousin offered a suggestion. "Why don't you guys visit the farm today?" Kimberly asked. "You and I can head up to Eastview Mall during the week since you've got a little time off. The weather's perfect, and I'm sure Brian won't mind if you come a day early. Once the baby's here, I'm going to be way less mobile with a newborn and a toddler. Does that work for you, Josie?"

Oh, it definitely worked for her, Josie decided. But while Kimberly's ploy wasn't clear to Jacob, Josie got it. And when Kimberly winked, out of sight from Jacob, the event planner's matchmaking instincts were loud and clear.

"We don't want to mess up your plans," Jacob began, but Josie stopped him.

"Kimberly's right. She and I can go shopping during the week, and this is Aunt Kate's last free weekend for a long time. She's stepping in while Kimberly's out with the baby, so sure." She aimed a smile down to Addie. "Today would be fine. Let me text Brian, just to be sure."

"And we can grab lunch somewhere, too, if that's all right?"

"You, sir, have found the way to any Gallagher heart," Kimberly assured him. "Food is always a great motivator."

"I figured anyone who creates a restaurant that shines in such a competitive market has to have a proper appreciation for food. The Carringtons made a smart move inviting Josie on board."

"Certainly better than having her open a spot

in the backyard." Cissy pointed to the for-sale sign on the hill overlooking the southern inn entrance.

"A possibility I pointed out to the COO," Jacob stage-whispered. "She was pretty mad."

"For good reason, all of which has been re-solved by good business," Josie informed both of them. She raised her phone. "Brian says it's fine for us to come on over."

"Awesome!" Addie clapped her hands, then hugged Josie tight around the waist. "I'm so excited to go visit them! Do I look all right?"

Did Addie look all right? She looked so be-yond all right that Josie had to work to find the right words. "You look perfect."

"Absolutely darling!" added Cissy, and Josie thought she might have sniffed when she said it, which meant they better hit the road because the last thing any of them needed was Cissy Gallagher dissolving into tears.

"Cooler than any one kid should be allowed to be," added Kimberly, and then she high-fived the youngster. "You've got your own style, kiddo. I like it."

"Thank you." Twin dimples appeared in Ad-die's cheeks, hiking the cute-as-can-be factor to an even higher degree.

"Let me touch base with Maybelle and the crew inside."

Jacob stepped away, withdrew his phone and spoke for a few moments, then rejoined them. "All set. Let's take my car, her booster's in the backseat."

Josie didn't make eye contact with her family. She just nodded in response, and when Addie grasped her hand—and then her father's—Josie knew how it looked. She also knew appearances were deceiving because the nice guy holding Addie's hand had no idea what was coming his way, and that didn't just make her feel bad. It made her feel terrible.

"I cannot even believe there are this many cows in the world." Eyes wide, Addie took in the mixed herd of red and black Angus cattle dotting the spring-green field stretching beyond Brian Gallagher's farmhouse. "This is so very amazing, Josie!"

"And your cousin runs the farm stand over there, too?" Jacob jutted his chin toward the Gallagher Farm Market.

"With the help of a Mennonite woman," she explained. "Martha watches the kids and does jams and jellies and baked goods for the market."

Brian's daughter Emily grabbed Addie's hand. "Can I take Addie to see the little goats out back?"

Josie almost said yes, then realized it wasn't her place to give permission. She pushed away the sting of realization and let Jacob take the lead. "Sure. Can we come along?"

"Yeah!" Emily and Addie raced ahead, laughing. The grown-ups followed with no need for speed.

"She's loving this, Josie."

"I know." Josie watched the girls duck around the corner of a near barn. "Brian's planting or he'd be here to say hello."

"To everything there is a season…"

"And a time for every purpose under the heaven." Josie finished the verse from Ecclesiastes. "I've always loved that verse. It speaks to the common-sense side of me."

"Me, too. When we lost Addie's mother, it was like our world turned upside down because no one expects that to happen. It was an 'out of season' event."

Josie held her breath. She wanted Jacob to talk about what happened, but digging for information felt wrong. "It's hard to lose someone so young."

His expression deepened. "My mom's still not over it. They're coming to visit soon, and I hope it helps. They miss Addie, my dad misses working, and they don't sound happy. When Ginger died, a void opened for them."

"Too many changes at once, maybe?"

He nodded. "And too little faith. When the lawyer said Ginger had left me custody of Addie, I couldn't believe it. My parents had raised us, they weren't elderly by any means, and they seemed insulted by the fact that a single guy was given custody of their only grandchild. But Ginger had left me a letter, explaining why she did it. And it made sense. I hated that my parents were hurt, but taking care of Addie was the least I could do for my sister. Addie had already survived so much…" He paused, thoughtful, watching the girls as they offered hay nuggets to the goats. "I owed it to her to do my best, and that's what I've done. And honestly?" Satisfaction marked his gaze. "I wouldn't have it any other way."

Josie picked her words carefully. "You said Addie survived so much…?"

He nodded. "She developed cancer as a toddler and had to have a liver transplant. Thankfully, the folks at Emory were able to find a match."

Emory hadn't found the match. Ginger did. Which meant she'd shaded the truth with Jacob, and that made Josie wonder what else his sister had lied about. "After the surgery she underwent follow-up treatments, none of which she really remembers, except for the farm animal murals on the walls of the children's rooms."

"Hence the love for cows, maybe?"

He acknowledged that possibility with a nod. "Could be. She was given up for adoption by a drug-using mother, but she's never shown a sign of problems, so we dodged a bullet on that one."

Drug-using mother?

Josie's chest went tight. Her throat followed. "She was adopted?"

"Yes. My sister said she was willing to take an at-risk baby for Addie's sake."

"She told you this?" Keeping her voice calm took every bit of strength Josie could muster.

He folded his hands on the top rail of the fencing as he watched the girls play. "Yes. I thought she was crazy because her marriage was falling apart, and I couldn't imagine why she wanted to bring a baby into all that drama, but in the end it worked out okay. In the short time they had together, she was a wonderful mother to Addie."

Anger didn't just pulse up Josie's spine, it thrummed a high, tight beat. He'd just confirmed her suspicions, that Ginger misrepresented their marriage to adopt Addie. And then to lie about Josie and call her a drug-using mother? Why would she do that?

Josie had been honest about her misguided experimentation with drugs after she lost her dad, but she'd been clean for a long time before Addie was conceived.

Her hands curled. Her palms went moist. She had to work to keep her face placid and pretend his story wasn't breaking her heart.

He believed his sister. Losing Ginger caused a lot of grief, but if she hadn't lied to the agency to begin with, none of this would have happened. Maybe she wouldn't have even been on that particular road that day... Who knew?

Ginger's misrepresentation began a chain of events that brought them to this moment, and while Josie loved the chance to see her daughter in person, she couldn't negate the truth. She and the agency had been intentionally duped. "Being a single parent isn't easy, I'm sure."

"It's the best thing that ever happened to me, actually." He faced her and flashed that sweet, endearing smile. "I used to bury myself in work, much like my father did. I'd gotten pretty one-dimensional. Then she came into my life." He grinned as Addie blew kisses to the crowd of goats, all begging for a treat. "She changed everything. I made a promise to myself and to God that I was going to make sure she had the most delightfully normal childhood any kid could have. And it's been good for both of us. She makes me remember to stop and smell the roses. Although in her case it's more like attending teddy bear picnics and teas and falling down while ice skating and going to the zoo on cold days to see if the Arctic animals are happy."

"I used to do that."

"Yeah?" He slanted a look her way, but she kept her gaze on Addie. Too much eye contact with Jacob deepened the conflict. Better to maintain a distance, but his caring nature made that difficult.

"My dad would take me into Rochester to check out the polar bears and seals and penguins. Everybody goes to the zoo in the summer, and the Arctic animals just kind of lay there, wondering what's going on. But in the winter, they seem so happy. So content."

"Dad!" Addie called his name in a bright voice laced with excitement. "Do you see this little brown-and-white goat? She likes me so much!"

"Well, you're quite lovable, so I'm not surprised."

Addie had climbed the lowest rung of fencing, just like Emily, and when she turned to look at Jacob, love and appreciation deepened her smile. "You too, Dad!"

Hurt knotted Josie's chest. She shouldn't envy

Addie's love for Jacob. She knew it was the best thing for Addie, and Jacob was devoted to her well-being. But to watch her declare her love for someone else, and have no idea her mother was standing nearby, didn't just prickle. It stabbed.

Take a breath. Remember your vow. You wanted the best for her, and watching her with Jacob, you know she's not just doing well, she's doing great. This is why you didn't do an open adoption, remember? You knew yourself well enough to make a clean break for her well-being.

Stow the anger and talk with Cruz. Today isn't about what happened six years ago. It's about now.

She took the advice seriously. What good was her original goal if she blew it out of the water six years later? She'd wanted a good life for Addie, and Jacob was providing that.

She'd deal with the old deceptions once Cruz had information for her, but from what Jacob had just revealed, Ginger O'Neill had connived her way to getting a child. How that would stand up legally—if she pressed—was anyone's guess.

"Addie? Are you getting hungry yet? Because I sure am."

"Yes." She hugged Emily and waved to the

cows. "I'll come see you again soon!" she promised, then raced to Jacob's side. "Dad, isn't this like the best day ever?"

"I cannot disagree with that assessment."

"Josie, thank you! Thank you so much for bringing me here!" Once again, she hugged Josie. And Josie bent and hugged her back.

She didn't want to let go.

Feeling Addie's arms around her, she longed to tell the child who she was and why she made the choices she did years before.

Of course, she did no such thing. She played it cool and fun, because like Jacob, she wanted Addie's life to be wonderful. How that would play out with the growing facts surrounding the adoption was anyone's guess, but she wasn't delving because Addie's situation concerned her. Jacob's love and devotion was all a child could ask for. She saw that clearly.

She was pursuing the matter because deception had surrounded Addie's conception. To have it dictate her adoption was like picking an old wound. It hit too many buttons.

Should that be Addie's problem?

No.

But it couldn't be ignored, either, because defrauding an adoption agency and a birth mother was no small thing. What would come of it? she wondered as they moved to the car.

She didn't know. But she wasn't going to stop gathering facts until she had the whole truth. And then—

Jacob laughed at something Addie said and scooped her up. He bumped his forehead to hers, and then they hugged...

She'd have to tell him. And despite what her mother cautioned, Josie was pretty sure he'd hate her for disrupting their sweet life.

Was she willing to take this further? Go to court?

Cruz had put that question to her, and she had no answers. Not yet. Witnessing Addie's complete comfort and joy today, maybe she'd have been smarter to just disappear for a while, until Jacob and Addie had moved on. Maybe God had provided her with that opportunity by selling her restaurant and having a significant bankroll for once in her life.

Now she'd signed a contract to stay.

Search me, O God, and know my heart: try me, and know my thoughts. The sweet words from the old psalm touched her.

She needed to step back and turn this over to God. Let him guide her way.

She hadn't prayed when she'd been offered that restaurant contract. She'd seized the chance to be near Addie like spring blooms seek sun after a long, drawn-out winter. She'd rushed, and maybe she shouldn't have.

It's never too late to pray, is it?

It wasn't. She knew that. But she also knew she'd acted quickly, and that wasn't like her. But when Addie reached out and grasped her hand as they crossed to Jacob's SUV, the touch of her daughter's fingers in hers made it all worthwhile.

Chapter Eight

"He said that to you?" Elbows propped on his desk, Cruz steepled his hands. "He told you his sister's marriage was falling apart?"

"In those very words."

Cruz noted something on a pad of paper. "Anything else?"

He looked up when Josie stayed quiet. When he spotted her tears, he pushed tissues her way. "Take your time."

She grabbed a stash of tissues and mopped her face, then took a moment to find her voice. "It's not a big deal, it's just…" She paused again. "She told him I was a drug user. She said she was adopting Addie from a drug-using mother because she wanted to help the child." Repeating the phrase brought another round of tears.

"Ginger was trying to justify her choices

when questioned," Cruz told her. "People who lie all the time get quite good at twisting the truth to suit their own ends."

"It brought everything back." Josie clutched the tissues tightly. "All my mistakes, and then how hard I tried to make the best decision I could for Addie."

"And you did."

"Well." She stood and slung her purse over her shoulder. "I thought you should know."

"I'll pass it along, but from what you've told me and what we know about the circumstances, I'd say you've got a strong case for litigation. Yes, she fooled the agency, too, but it's their job to screen thoroughly. If her brother was aware the marriage was in trouble, then maybe people should have checked deeper into their references."

"You mean sue the agency?"

He nodded.

"I don't want money, Cruz." She worked the tissues in her left hand like one of those squeezable therapy balls. "I want them to be more careful, I want them to know what happened, but I don't want money. Right now, I want the one thing I gave up a long time ago." She breathed deep. "My little girl. But what mother can justify tearing her child's life apart for her own desires?" She didn't wait for Cruz to answer because there really was no answer. "Kiss Rory and those kids for me."

"I will. And I'll be in touch when I hear back from Cait."

"Okay." She walked out into the cooling, late-day air. She hadn't planned on seeing Cruz today, but when she saw the glow of his office light through the window, she'd walked in.

Her phone signaled a text. Kimberly, wondering if she wanted to talk.

She didn't want to talk. She barely wanted to think. She'd spent hours that day with the most precious gift of all, and instead of being grateful for that opportunity, she wanted more. Much more.

Exactly what she couldn't have.

"Do I look nice?" Addie preened in front of the mirror nearly a week later. "Memaw likes hats, Dad. Should I wear one?" She popped a jaunty cap onto her copper hair and looked like something out of a pricey kids' clothing magazine.

"You look great, and Memaw loves you no matter what you wear."

"But she does like people to look *just so*. She told me that one day," she reminded him. "I think it means extra nice."

"Well, in that case, I think you look 'just

so' every single minute of every single day, so we've got that covered." He knew what she meant, though. His mother's outlook on things wasn't bad, but she'd been skewed by money for a long time. For her, "just so" took on a new connotation. "And I think they just pulled in."

"For real?" Addie raced to the door, no longer caring about the perfect look, and when his father hauled her up into his arms, Jacob knew the visit was well-timed. "Oh, Pawpaw," Addie wrapped her arms around her grandfather's neck and held on tight. "I missed you and Memaw so much. Look how big I am now!" She leaned back to allow his father a proper look. "And we went ice skating and sledding and it was cold, but not too cold," she assured him, shaking her head and laughing as if he might worry about the temperature. "I think you should come visit us here in the winter, and see the snow and we could do things together, okay?"

"Visit you in the winter?" His mother seized the words quickly. "Are you staying on up here for another winter, Jacob?"

He hugged his mother, then kept an arm wrapped around her shoulders. She felt thinner, and he didn't like that because she wasn't a big woman in the first place. "Addie's decided she loves the town and the schools and just about everything you can name here in Grace Haven, but I've reminded her that I actually need a job, so we're exploring options for the coming year."

"This is my first, second and third opi-shun," she told his father, holding up three fingers as she fumbled the word. "I don't even think we need more than that, do we?"

His father laughed and hugged her close. "I've missed you, kid. Memaw and I were just saying we don't want to spend another five months apart, it's far too long. Jacob, how's the project going? Wrapping up on something this big can be a fun and exhausting time."

"You're right about that," Jacob admitted. "The mistakes are a headache, but then I get to fix them, and that's what they pay me for. And so far, so good, I'm pleased with how things are going, which means the Carringtons are pleased."

"Job security, right there."

Jacob hesitated. "I'm indecisive at the moment."

"You haven't been indecisive since you learned how to crawl." His father studied him more closely. "You started by moving forward and that's what you've done, every step of the way. I didn't think the word existed in your vocabulary."

"Well, it's different now." He grinned at Addie in his father's arms, but didn't want to say too much. First, Addie was right there. Second, tweaking his mother's consternation about being bypassed to raise her granddaughter wouldn't make for a fun time.

"So Addie's still in school?" his mother asked. She hugged Addie while his dad held her, a sweet image of family unity. Maybe a unity they could have again, someday. "Schools down south were out weeks ago."

"School lets out later up here. It starts later, too, but they're not doing too much right now." He aimed a teasing look at Addie, a look he shared with his mother. "Were you hoping to spend the day together?"

"I sure was!" Addie punched her hand into the air. "Dad, can we do that for real? Have a day with Memaw and Pawpaw?"

"You can." He made a face of regret. "I'm working. We've got Josie's kitchen put together enough for her to get the smoker up and running, so while the kitchen crew gets assembled for the take-out shack, I'll be overseeing grounds and parking lot details. And the penthouse floor."

"A far-flung focus right there," his father noted.

"The brisket from the barbecue restaurant

will be my reward at the end of the day. You guys don't mind taking charge of my best girl?"

"Mind?" His dad hugged Addie closer. "We'll consider it an honor."

"Then I'll see you tonight. You got settled into your lake house all right?"

"Your mother loves it, and that's half the battle." His father was teasing, but earned a dour look from his mom. "It's got everything we need, including basic groceries. And did you know the store in town delivers?"

Jacob did know that, but most folks ran into Grace Haven to get their own groceries. "It's an amazing convenience."

"I'll say." His mother touched his arm, then stepped away. "We don't want to hold you up from work."

"See ya." He hugged Addie. "Have fun, squirt. Show Memaw and Pawpaw all your favorite places, okay?"

"Okay, Dad!"

They headed off, three adventurers, on a quest for fun. His mother had noticed Addie's voice at Christmas, how a northern twang seemed to be replacing her Southern drawl. And who would have expected a child Addie's age to fall in love with a place? A theme park, yes. He got that. But a town? A way of life? And yet Addie had taken to this northern town as if born to it, but his mother wouldn't like the idea of their being so far away. She'd already lost so much. Too much.

He put his thoughts on hold as he pulled into the lower parking lot of the inn a short while later. Most of the construction tape had been removed, allowing better access to all four sides of the sprawling building. He got out of his car, and the first thing that struck him was the scent of smoking meat, but along with the scent came an image... Not of barbecue, but of the woman creating the barbecue.

He cut through the nearly finished lobby, ducked through the deliberately down-scaled Bayou Barbecue and paused when he spotted Josie. She was demonstrating smoking techniques to a rapt group of construction guys. She'd braided her hair. Pulled back, it accentuated her profile, the high cheekbones and expressive eyes.

Alive in beauty.

He wasn't generally the most expressive of men, but the phrase came to him, watching her.

The crew listened as Josie explained what she was doing with the multilayer smoker. It wasn't her lesson that stopped Jacob. It was the look of interest in a tall, dark-haired carpenter's eye as she explained her process.

His chest went tight. His jaw firmed, and it

was all he could do to keep from rolling back his shoulders in challenge. He purposely shut the emotion down as he pushed through the screened door separating the kitchen from the newly covered and vented smoker area, trying to sound casual when he might actually prefer to stake a claim, nice and loud. Except he had no claim. "How's it working?"

Josie looked up quickly. She smiled just as quick, and when she did, a spark of interest that went beyond business brightened her gaze. Or maybe it was wishful thinking on his part. But when their eyes met again, it wasn't wishful thinking that made her tuck a wisp of hair back, behind her ear, watching him. "It's amazing, Jacob. The guys did a great job putting it together, and once we tweaked the vent levers, I had wonderful control of the timing process."

"Well, that venting brought me this way." He didn't mention the second reason he hurried through the spacious hotel entrance. "Is this the practice session?"

"Yes. I was telling the guys we'll do sandwiches for the crew later on. I'm going to fill the roaster oven with Idaho potatoes, too, so we can have everything synchronized for the take-out shack."

"Looks great, Josie." One of the crew tipped

his hat as he went off to work. "Let us know when the dinner gong goes off."

"Gladly, Rick," she called as she readjusted a small vent on one end. "By the end of this week, I want to know this machine from top to bottom. Temperature variations are part of the scientific equation."

"Gotta love a woman who can mix science with great 'cue." It was the dark-haired carpenter who spoke, and Jacob was relieved when Josie barely glanced up to acknowledge him.

He waited until the guy walked away and Josie had straightened. "Let me know if you need anything adjusted, okay? We can get the guys right on it."

"I will, Jacob." She looked up again. She was wearing a dark green tank top and capris. She'd tossed her chef's jacket onto the stone wall, another clue that Josie Gallagher didn't always follow the rules. "Maybe you and Addie can stop by for food later, too."

"She'd love the baked potatoes and toppings, but she's out with my parents today. They arrived late yesterday, and Addie is already filling them in on the town, her intentions to stay and why it's the perfect place in the world, which may have something to do with your cousin's cows."

"She wants to stay?" Josie faced him fully,

and he'd have to be blind to miss the new concern in her expression and Jacob had excellent vision. So what was it that could possibly bother her? "Here?"

"Well, she's six, so the realities of job procurement are somewhat lost on her." He grinned. "She considers that a minor detail, but yes. She now considers Grace Haven her home."

"It's a wonderful town. And a great place to raise a family," Josie told him, but she looked more sad than happy. "A lot of the Gallagher clan settled in the area, so we can relate to Addie's fondness."

His phone rang.

He wanted to ignore it.

He wanted to ask what put that note of melancholy in her eyes, but she moved back into the kitchen.

He answered the phone, and for the next several hours he was caught up in the busyness of overseeing the overseers. And when Maybelle arrived midafternoon to check the kitchen detailing in all four restaurants, he ran into her at the upscale Eastern Shore Steak Company on the second floor, angled with a curved and stunning view of the water and the rolling hills beyond. "How does the steakhouse look, Maybelle?"

She handed him a short list. "A few things to tweak, and the sooner the better so your fancy chef with an attitude doesn't come down on you like a swatter on a fly."

"Apt analogy." He pocketed the list. "And the other spots?"

"Josie's got her hand in that barbecue already, and the room's not quite done, so if the health inspector wanders by, make sure no one's cutting dry wall while she's stirring sauce or making chili, all right? That girl's more ambitious than most, and it's so good to see her up here in her own element, doin' fine. Just fine."

The heartiness in her observation tweaked him. "Is there a reason she wouldn't be doing fine?" It wasn't Maybelle's response, but her face that said there might be more than she was saying.

"It's a tough business to get into, and she's got tenacity." Maybelle shrugged. "And that's all I'm sayin'."

And yet her expression continued to indicate there was more to the story.

"The downstairs café is all set to go except for the tables, and the sandwich bar refrigerator unit isn't the one I ordered," she told him. "I know it's a fuss, but there's a reason I ordered the larger unit with better compression."

"I'll have it switched out within the week. Did you see the smoker?"

"I surely did, and the pride and joy in Josie's eyes when she showed it to me." Maybelle patted his shoulder. "Your men did well, that's the cornerstone of a great barbecue. To have a grand old smoker and a cook who is not afraid to use it. She said you're planning a smaller version for catering gigs. That's all the rage right now, so it's a smart move, Jacob. I'll tell Marv Carrington that when I see him, but I expect it was your call. You see a lot more than most job supers do, and when it comes to restaurant creation, you are your daddy's boy." She started for the door. "Call if you need to, I've got to check on a kitchen just outside of DC, and you know folks with mansions. They need to have the best of everything in a room they generally never see. But it will be a cook's dream."

"I expect it will." He didn't say he understood that reasoning better than most. The thought of his mother cooking was more fairy tale than fact, but his father loved to cook, so it worked out.

But when they were growing up his father was gone long hours. Days, sometimes weeks, creating his brand and hosting grand openings. Sheila Weatherly had brought the kids to attend many of them, but as he and Ginger matured, conflicting schedules were the rule of the day. Maybe having a cook and a housekeeper wasn't an indulgence. Perhaps it simply allowed his mother to be present at all those other things. Ball games and dance recitals and tennis matches for Ginger.

He'd always thought his mother was a little spoiled, and maybe she was, in a way. But perhaps she was doing what she needed to do to be a good wife and a great mother.

That made the slap in the face sharper when the lawyer read Ginger's will out loud. His sister's choice had hurt his mother, and when he wouldn't sign Addie over to his parents, a rift had formed. It was better now…but not fully healed. He wanted that healing. He wanted anguish and grief and hurt feelings to be old news. Addie deserved to be surrounded by positive emotions. She'd had more turmoil than any young child should ever endure.

He came down the main stairway, checking things as he moved. A glorious lobby rose up to an overarching ceiling. The massive chandelier had been completed, and the entire effect welcomed guests to something bigger and bolder than they'd seen on the lake before. And yet, tucked to the northern edge, was a local treasure, a barbecue dive to draw in locals while the steak house upstairs might be preferred by some of the inn's more formal guests and business functions.

Either way, this newest Carrington resort was his favorite. He spotted Josie moving toward a side door and called her name. "Got a minute?"

She moved his way. She should look out of place with her tank top and light khaki capris, but she didn't, and he realized she had just enough moxie to fit in anywhere, a quality he admired. "Just," she told him. "My cousin is in labor and my mom and I are watching little Davy while she's in the hospital. Mom's on her way here now. She's having an old hardwood floor refinished today. For the moment, her house is uninhabitable."

"Want a coffee while we wait for her?"

"I never say no to coffee. Especially on someone else's dime. And while I offer a true Louisiana chicory mix for customers who've acquired a taste for the stuff, I need coffee that tastes like coffee." She fell into step beside him, and he couldn't help himself. He leaned over and sniffed, on purpose.

She laughed. "I know, I smell like smoke and seasonings and all things Cajun and Southern right now. Hazards of the trade. Sorry."

"Wasn't complaining, ma'am. More like appreciating."

Color rose to her cheeks. Not pink like fairer

skin would show, but a deep rose that blended with her tawnier complexion. "So, back to coffee." She aimed a firm look to quash his flirting, which only made him want to flirt more. "I put a one-cup dispenser into the kitchen this morning, with a big—" she stretched her arms wide "—box of pods because when it comes to coffee, this New Yorker doesn't mess around."

"Nor does the Southern gentleman by your side." He held the door open to the first-floor administrative office suite. "Is your mother going to be here for a little while?"

"Not by choice, but yes." She followed him to the sophisticated but visually simple coffee machine in the second room. "She can't have the little guy at her house right now, and of course Aunt Kate is at the hospital. It's too nice a day to send them to my apartment, and Davy will love the beach. I figured I'd feed Mom, and she can watch Davy play in the sand until I'm cleaned up and out of here. A beautiful day like today shouldn't be taken for granted."

"I'm not sure I appreciated 'soft weather' like I should have in the past," he acknowledged as he pulled out his phone. "And while I didn't mind the winter, I didn't mind seeing it end, either. Now I get where the phrase came from."

"Wishing winter over is a common observance up here, but you didn't run screaming, so that's a plus."

He smiled. "I'll call my parents and see if they can bring Addie back here for food. She's a born potato lover. Doesn't matter how we fix them, Addie's on board." He hit speed dial and the speaker icon as he maneuvered the coffee machine. "Hey, Mom, you there?"

His mother sounded a little out of breath. "Do you know how big the hills are here, Jacob?"

He laughed because Addie would live in the hills if he let her. "I do. And Addie wants to climb every one. Has she tired you out?"

"Energized us is more like it!" his father's voice boomed in, which meant he was on speaker, too. "And we've worked up an appetite, sure enough!"

"My father talks in exclamation points, much like Addie," Jacob whispered with his hand over the sensitive phone mic. "Dad, one of our new restaurants has a food spread on. Why don't you guys come back here for supper, and we can take Addie into town for custard later. She can show you all her favorites."

"Are you talking barbecue, son? Because don't tease a Southern man with some ill-famed edition of Yankee barbecue. I'm no one's fool when it comes to good 'cue, and you know that."

Jacob winced because Josie was standing right there, hearing every word, but when Josie answered, he was pretty sure she'd stand her ground with his father. And possibly win. "I will throw down the gauntlet to you, Mr. Weatherly, because my 'cue will stand up to the best of the best in the Deep South, and/or Southwest, take your pick. Unless you're going to pretend that the Carolinas have anything up their sleeves to compete with the Gulf. Because I'm pretty sure you know they don't. At least that's the word in Cajun country."

A long, slow silence ensued, until his father burst out laughing. "I'll take up your challenge, young woman, and all the cheek in this world won't change my mind if your food doesn't stand the test. Although I'll do my best to be polite."

Josie laughed.

So did his father.

And just like that they'd met on some indefinable restaurant-friendly common ground. Jacob wasn't sure what he'd do if his father didn't like Josie's barbecue, and Bob Weatherly wasn't exactly discreet. If something needed work, he let you know in no uncertain terms. But hearing Josie go toe-to-toe with his father had done something he hadn't been able to do the past couple of years.

She made his father sound like the old Robert Weatherly, the proud and funny CEO of a major restaurant chain, at the top of his game.

He hung up the phone and turned her way. She'd finished brewing her coffee, and added a generous shot of syrup, then foamed milk to the top. "This—" she lifted her cup and her gaze "—is the most amazing coffee machine ever."

Their eyes locked, and suddenly he wasn't thinking about coffee, or his dad, or anything except the attractive and amazing woman in front of him.

Strong. Kind. Resolute. She'd gone the distance with corporate offices and came out a winner, and Jacob had been in this business long enough to understand the rarity in that.

But it wasn't her business acumen calling him. Or the smoke-scented hair and clothing.

It was her—the strong, beautiful woman who hid her wounds well, and wore a sea-green tank top like other women wore designer labels.

He leaned forward, his gaze traveling from her eyes to her lips, wondering, and not wanting to wonder anymore.

And she leaned forward, too.

Then she drew back. "Um. No."

Jacob didn't draw back. "I think yes."

She stepped away and indicated the coffee.

"I'm grateful for the coffee, but that's as far as this goes. I don't kiss casually, I don't flirt and I'm not into short-term relationships, so let's call an immediate halt to this attraction."

"So the lady admits there's an attraction."

"The lady also states that the attraction is to be avoided." She faced him frankly and kept her voice firm. "She is not a fan of broken hearts or messing up little kids' lives with transient affections. You're leaving in another month. I'm staying here with a brand-new business to run. Complicating matters isn't in the schedule."

"What if they're already complicated?" he asked.

She stayed quiet, walked through the office door and didn't turn. As stated, she didn't flirt, although he'd given her the perfect opening. She moved straight on through the restaurant to the smoker area while he followed.

"Josie! We're here!" Her mother's voice interrupted the conversation from across the paved lot. She waved once she'd lifted Kimberly's little guy out of a car seat. "And Davy's so excited to go play in the sand!"

Jacob's parents' car pulled in and parked right next to Josie's mother. They climbed out, looking happier than he'd seen them in a long time. Time with Addie did that to people. She brought out the best in folks.

Addie hopped out, looked around the parking lot like he'd taught her to do, and headed toward Josie's mother. "Are you guys here to see Josie? Who is this little guy? This is my Memaw, right here!" She grabbed hold of his mother's hand and drew her forward, and her excitement put more joy in his mother's face than he'd seen in a long while. "And my Pawpaw! This is Josie's mother. I met her the other day!"

She spoke as if excited by life, but while his mother appeared delighted, Josie's mother was suddenly fighting tears.

Two strange reactions to Addie in one day. Like mother, like daughter?

He started forward, but Josie intercepted her mother quickly. "Mom, I know this whole having-babies thing gets the entire Gallagher clan emotional, and I'm glad you were able to bring Davy over. I see you brought his sand bucket of toys. Perfect!" She stayed matter-of-fact, so Jacob did the same. "Mr. Weatherly. Mrs. Weatherly." Josie stuck out her hand to his parents in turn. "A pleasure to make your acquaintance. Jacob has talked about you both, and how you inspired him from the time he was little." She shook their hands, holding his father's hand for extra beats of the clock. "And while I may have tweaked you on the phone, sir, if you have any advice to offer once you've had supper, I'd love to hear it. It isn't every day I get to chat with one of the great icons in restaurant history."

"Flattery will get you everywhere, my dear." Jacob's father grinned and clapped her on the back gently. "I don't get the chance to talk business much anymore. I miss it."

"Retirement isn't exactly what we thought it would be, that's for sure." His mother didn't look combative; a welcome change. She'd pushed for the Florida move, longing for something with no memories of her lost daughter dogging every step she took, but she clearly wasn't all that happy with the new reality, either.

"Are you guys going to the beach?" Addie asked. She danced on her toes, excited. "I would love to do that! Can I, Dad? Can I go to the beach with Josie's mom and the little guy?"

"This is Davy." Josie palmed the little fellow's cheek with one tawny hand. "His mom's having a baby, so he's staying with my mom for a couple of days."

"Oh, I want a baby brother or sister someday." Addie's eyes went round. She clasped both hands over her heart. "That is my best wish ever, Josie." Gazing up, imploring, she carried the little-girl drama to the hilt. "To have my dad find someone to marry and we can have little brothers and sisters and be a big, happy family!"

Chapter Nine

"Hey." Jacob pretended to be affronted as he bent to Addie's level. "Kid. I'm pretty sure we're happy, right?"

Addie nodded.

"Then let's leave the wedding thing in God's hands, okay?"

Addie rolled her eyes. "I guess."

Josie's heart didn't just crumble. It shattered into a million tiny, silent pieces, hearing her daughter's wishes and dreams.

Addie wanted normal.

Addie longed for a mother, not knowing her mother stood before her.

And here was Cissy Gallagher, about to cry her eyes out because she couldn't acknowledge her granddaughter while Addie heaped love on Jacob's parents.

How in the world had she ever thought staying around was a good idea? *Dumb, Josie. Plain dumb.*

"I'll walk down with you, if that's all right?" Sheila motioned toward the beach. "I'd love to have some time to tuck my toes in the sand and watch the kids play."

Josie's mother had recovered enough to swipe a hand to her eyes and nod, but would she be all right on the beach with Jacob's mother while Josie worked? Or would Cissy feel a sudden need to bear her heart and soul to the other woman and possibly incite a new war of northern aggression? Josie had to trust she'd keep her feelings to herself.

"I'd love to have a look around the resort, son." Mr. Weatherly spoke up as the women and kids walked toward the hotel's front.

"Sure." She felt Jacob's eyes on her, but she didn't look up. She checked the temps on the smoker before going back inside, and when the men also moved toward the front of the expansive resort hotel, she let the tears come.

What was she doing here? Not just in the hotel, but in Grace Haven at all? Why hadn't she run away when Addie first appeared?

Because Addie was with the wrong person, that's why, only he might be the right person, after all. Certainly more right than the pretend father who deserted his marriage once the adoption was complete. Or the mother who lied her way through agency protocol to gain a child.

Emotions didn't just hit her, they ransacked, and just as she decided she might pull out some chicken and give it a thorough pounding to release her aggression, her phone rang. Cruz's name came up on the display. She drew a deep breath to gain control of her rolling emotions and answered. "Cruz. What's up?"

"Can you talk?"

She glanced around and nodded. "Yes."

"Adam O'Neill signed over full custody of Addie before their divorce was final. Before the six-month statute and their finalized application in front of a judge. Between what you heard from Jacob, and this proof that I'm sure Ginger never thought would be found, it's clear that they misrepresented themselves to the agency to gain a child."

So it was true. Jacob's sister maneuvered her husband and her situation to adopt Addie.

"This changes things, Josie."

Josie wasn't so sure. "It clears things up, but what can it change, Cruz? Do I move forward out of some misplaced anger and mess up a child's life because I was wronged? Or do I think about King Solomon and his ruling, that a child should be divided to satisfy two fighting women? If you truly love someone, how can you intentionally tear them apart?"

"I hear what you're saying." Cruz spoke deliberately, the way he often did. "But there was a crime committed here, Josie. So yes, it's worked out all right, and I'm glad about that, but it could be argued that the original crime of misrepresentation could have egregious effects on the child. She never had a father to speak of, and the mother was taken out of the picture through no fault of her own. However, her original deceit left Addie orphaned, which can have its own emotional stamp on a child's life. The initial lie or misrepresentation then becomes the catalyst for the ensuing result. Before you make any decisions, think about that, all right?"

"I will. I wish…" She sighed, choking down emotion once again.

"That this had never happened."

She drew a breath and swiped a kitchen towel to her eyes. "Yes. And this beautiful child's life wasn't comprised of deception upon deception. That's so wrong, Cruz. And yet…"

"Yes?"

"She seems happy. And content. I can't in good conscience mess that up. I'm delighted to see her happy. I rejoice in that."

"Except…"

She didn't try to hold back the sigh. "A part of me is filled with this longing to be her mother. But I have to push that part aside."

"Don't hurry your decisions, take some time to digest all of this," Cruz advised. "The agency is appalled by the way, and you'll probably be hearing from their attorney."

More people knowing.

The walls began to close in around her. "Tell them they don't need to. Tell them—"

"I can't, Josie. I can't tell them what to do. They understand your plight, but they need to cover themselves legally. They bear the ultimate responsibility for what's happened, and they're pretty sure you're about to sue them for a whole lot of money."

"Sue them?" This couldn't get worse. "I'm not suing anyone, I just..." She paused for breath, thoroughly rattled. "I want my daughter safe and sound. And yes, I'm thoroughly ticked off that someone got around the system, and the fact that the agency didn't catch on to the O'Neills' plans infuriates me because if Jacob knew about it, others must have known, too. Should he have come forward and told the agency? Did they even talk to him? And does this mean that the O'Neills' references lied? How much can an agency be expected to do?" The intentionally tangled web infuriated her. "So maybe they didn't do their best home-work in this case. Maybe the fact that Ginger and Adam had plenty of money to finance the adoption meant they didn't get looked at very closely. And that's enough to anger anyone, isn't it?"

"I concur. Think about it. Digest it. It's a lot to take in. And Josie?"

"Yes?"

"I'm sorry. I can't tell you in words how sorry I am because you did nothing wrong and everything right. It wasn't you that failed. It was the system. And I'd be lying if I pretended that the legal side of me doesn't want the system to pay."

"I know. Thank you, Cruz." She hung up the phone. If she was home, she'd have plunked herself onto the couch and had a good cry, but she wasn't home. She was here, working under the same roof as Addie's father, having her heart wrenched more every day.

Focus on faith and work. On the good and not the bad. You can do this. You've done it before, remember?

She did remember, and she could do it again. She would do it again, because saving face for Addie meant more than getting even ever could. It meant everything.

* * *

Jacob watched his father taste the various foods on his plate, bite by bite, and when his father finally grinned and doffed his baseball cap in Josie's honor, Jacob breathed a sigh of relief.

"I hereby name you the Queen of Barbecue, Miss Gallagher. Whatever it is you've done, and whoever you've worked with or studied under, this is an exemplary job. If I was running a restaurant business at this moment, it would revolve around your food."

"Oh, you're a Southern schmoozer." Josie laughed as she swiped a napkin to little Davy's cheek. "Jacob didn't prepare me for that."

"Except he's not," Sheila assured her. "If there is one credit and one fault in my husband, it's that he speaks his mind, sometimes when the occasion does not warrant a spoken mind."

They all laughed.

"But he's right about this, Josie. This brisket, these ribs." She pinched her thumb and forefinger together and raised them to her lips. "Perfection."

"Well." Josie managed to look pleased and bothered by the accolades. "Thank you."

"You're most welcome. What's your thought on corn bread or spoon bread?"

Jacob watched as Josie and his father discussed the merits of menu choices. Josie's mother hadn't eaten much, and when Addie was done, she and Cissy Gallagher had taken a walk up the beach. Addie had been dashing back and forth through the sand, searching for beach treasures, but as they drew closer, his daughter paused, reached out and clasped Cissy's hand.

Addie looked up at the older woman.

Josie's mother looked down. And in that moment, their profiles reflected one another, as if made from the same mold. And it wasn't the accidents of coloration, the strawberry blond hair, green eyes and freckles.

The shape of their heads, gazing at each other, made them look more alike.

Then Addie released Cissy's hand so she could race their way. "Wait till you see what we found on the shore, it's so cool! And Mrs. Gallagher said if we drive up to Lake Ontario sometime, there's all kinds of treasures on the beach because big waves come crashing in and throw stuff onto the shore. Can we, Dad? Can we go to that beach sometime?"

"It's only an hour's drive," his father added. "Your mother and I created a list of things we'd like to see while we're here, and the Great Lakes are beautiful."

"And very different from this," Josie told them. She stood as her mother drew closer.

"I've got to finish the kitchen cleanup so Mom and I can take Davy home before he goes into meltdown mode. And hopefully we'll soon be hearing about another little one joining the fold."

"Do you know if it's a boy or a girl?" Sheila asked, and he was surprised when it took Cissy a few long beats to answer. Josie jumped into the gap.

"A girl this time."

"Oh, how sweet." Sheila beamed. "It's a joy raising both, of course, but there is nothing like shopping for a little girl, is there? The colors? The frill and the fluff?"

"I expect it's amazing, Sheila." Cissy shifted her gaze from Addie to Jacob's mother. "Absolutely amazing."

"I'll help get things in order." Jacob stood, and when Josie began to wave him off, he wouldn't let her. "I said I'll help." She tried not to meet his gaze, but then she did, and there it was again. The background sadness in her eyes, the hint of something wrong. So wrong. But when she pitched a towel at him in the kitchen, she'd masked the look, and that made him wonder why she had so much practice masking the look.

She'd done the major cleanup before they sat down to eat, and once the food had been stowed and the last pots washed, she surveyed the kitchen around them. "This is like a dream come true, Jacob. This kitchen. This setting."

"I'm glad you like it, Josie. But—"

She looked up, expecting a more businesslike thought than he was about to offer.

"I wish I knew what was making you sad. I wish I could help. I'd like to help," he finished. He didn't touch her, but he wanted to touch her. He wanted to draw her into his arms, against his heart, and tell her everything would be okay, but these were uncharted waters for him.

She shrugged as if it was no big deal. "Just tired. Busy days, a lot of planning and too much thinking. But thank you."

She started to move away.

He paused her with one hand. "If you ever want to talk, I'm here. Okay?"

She didn't look up this time. She kept her gaze down and nodded, then moved forward, away from his touch, his words. Away from him.

She'd warned him off earlier for good reason. He was moving on with his life, with his job, and she was staying here, but as she walked outside, another emotion jabbed him.

He didn't like seeing her walk away. It took a strong will not to chase after her, to walk side by side.

A call came in from a downstate supplier, and by the time he'd handled business, Josie and her mother had taken little Davy home.

His father came to meet him once he'd locked up. "We had a nice day, son. Real nice." He smiled as Jacob's mom and Addie blew bubbles and chased them along the sand. "I haven't seen your mother this happy in a long time. Not since we lost your sister," he added. "Ginger had her faults, and your mom was quick to get her out of scrapes, but when you love a child it's hard to sit back and watch them suffer. Even if it's from their own choices."

"I've come to realize that parenting looks a lot easier than it is, especially when you have good parents setting the example," Jacob admitted. "But it's also more rewarding than I ever imagined."

"There's that, for certain. Although I look back and wish I'd been around more. Sometimes a man needs to just kick back and be a dad, but in our day, if the man was working and the woman took over, it generally worked out."

"It did work out, Dad. You were an awesome father," Jacob assured him. "We understood you needed to work, and Mom was always on board. Honestly, two kids couldn't have asked for better parents. Ginger was just—" He wavered and chose his words carefully. "Needier."

"And more conniving," admitted his father. "With you, I always knew where you stood, what your plans were, what direction you aimed for. Your sister would say one thing and do another, and while it wasn't anything I'd call sinister, she wasn't afraid to double-deal folks, either. I think we spoiled her when she was young, when she had that bad bout of illness, then kept on spoiling her because we were so glad she lived."

Now that he was a father, Jacob understood how easily that could happen. "I thank God for Addie every day," he confessed. "Knowing what she went through, knowing what her life could have been like with a drug-using mother, and seeing how everything came together to bring her to us. We're blessed that she survived the cancer, that she's ours and that she's so gifted. Her life could have been so different if she hadn't become part of our family."

"It took a lot of courage for that mother to have her, then give her up," his dad said. "That's got to be about the hardest thing there is, don't you think? Especially when some people make other choices these days."

Jacob couldn't cut Addie's birth mother that kind of slack. "There's not much nobility in taking drugs while you're pregnant, Dad. But I'm glad Addie's okay. I mean, she's better than okay. She's amazing. And time to change the subject because our gals are heading this way."

"Agreed." They walked forward to meet Sheila and Addie, and when she leaped into Jacob's arms, he pretended to be overwhelmed by her size, and staged a pratfall.

She laughed and hung on tight, and that's how it had been from the first time he held her. He'd recognized the precious gift from God right away, almost as if it was somehow meant to be…and he'd been cherishing that gift every day since.

Chapter Ten

The five-day countdown was on.

Josie posted lists on the restaurant wall to prepare everyone for their quiet opening, three days prior to the grand affair. The quiet opening would help catch glitches in the system, in food, in production, to ensure the true opening would go off without a snag.

Her kitchen staff was in place, wait staff was being trained and the take-out shack had been busy from the day it opened, which meant she'd been back to work full-time and organizing the game plan for the new restaurant part-time for two weeks.

It kept her busy, and being busy had kept her sane.

She thanked God for that every day, because when she was busy, she didn't spend time thinking of the quickly moving calendar, racing toward a time when Jacob and Addie would move on to another place, another time.

Drew had given Jacob the all clear from a law enforcement perspective, but she hadn't needed his official report to know what kind of person Jacob was. Seeing him with her daughter, with his parents, with coworkers—she not only witnessed the good, kind, faith-filled actions, she admired them and liked them. Too much, actually.

She steered clear of him deliberately, but when Addie was around, she couldn't help staying nearby as their time together grew shorter. When she spotted Addie hunched on an outside bench that morning with red-rimmed eyes and damp cheeks, she couldn't just walk by. "Hey. What's up, Miss Weatherly?"

Addie said nothing as more silent tears rolled down her sweet, fair cheeks. Josie sank down onto the bench next to her as Jacob approached with a handful of tissues. "What's going on?"

"The school is hosting a mother/daughter event this morning. It's an annual tradition for the last week of classes and my mother was going to go with Addie, but she came down with that stomach bug during the night, so Mom isn't in any shape to go anywhere. Addie's really disappointed."

"But you can go. Right? I know you've got a lot to oversee, but—"

"Daddy always comes to stuff, Josie. He likes coming." Addie lifted watery eyes to Jacob and tried to smile. "But whenever there's something for a mom, I never have one. And all the other kids do. I was just so excited that Memaw was coming because it would be almost like having a mom with me." Twin tears slipped down her cheeks, onto her calico peasant shirt. "Because then I'd kind of be like the other kids."

Oh, her heart.

How could she take this barrage on a vital organ? She stared into the most beautiful eyes she'd ever known, the sweetest face she'd ever seen, and couldn't help herself. "May I come?"

Addie's eyes went wide as she lifted her brows in surprise. "Would you do that?"

She shouldn't. Every internal warning system a woman possessed was going off inside her, but when would she ever have such a chance again? Never. "It would be my pleasure. Just let me brief Terry on what's going on today. He needs to fly solo as backup manager, and this would give him the perfect opportunity. And, of course, all of this depends on if it's all right with your father…"

"It would be wonderful to have you there with us, Josie," Jacob assured her.

"Us?"

Addie nodded as she hopped off the bench and clutched both of their hands. "Dad's coming, too. He likes to be at things with me, but Josie, that would be so special. Thank you!" Then she let go of their hands and threw her arms around Josie in the biggest, sweetest hug Josie could imagine. "I'm so glad you're coming!"

"Me, too."

Nearly two weeks of avoiding him, and here she was, spending the morning with him and Addie. She gave Terry a quick rundown and then settled herself in Jacob's front seat.

The cushy car wrapped itself around her. Leather seats felt cool despite the rising outdoor temps, and as he drove toward Addie's school, his scent wandered her way. Woodsy, tangy and a hint of citrus, maybe? A marvelous scent that invited further inspection, a temptation she resisted.

The morning flew.

Josie wanted it to last forever.

It didn't. The teacher had orchestrated crafts for them to do together. They colored construction paper bookmarks and planted bright pink petunias into wide, foam coffee cups. They played silly games, then had a fairly minor-league tea party at the end, but Addie loved every single minute. And when it was over, she clasped onto Josie as if she'd never wanted to let her go, a sentiment Josie reciprocated. "Thank you so much for coming! Wasn't it the best day ever?"

More than she would ever know, and far more than Josie could ever put into words. "It sure was, and I'm so glad you guys let me come. It was by far the best day ever."

"Then let's not end it here." Jacob took Addie's hand as they crossed the parking lot to his car. "It's a gorgeous day and I promised Addie a trip to Lake Ontario. Let's do it now, before the resort opens, school closes for the summer and the beaches get crowded. Terry's got the Bayou kitchen covered, I can handle anything I need to via phone for the day, and we've already played hooky for the morning. Why not make it a whole day? I do believe there's custard at the Charlotte beach up in Rochester."

"There is," Josie admitted. "And there's a carousel, too. It's over a hundred years old, and so old-fashioned and pretty."

"Can we go? Please?" Addie implored as she reached for Josie's hand. "Will you come with us, Josie? That would make it even more special."

What kind of mother could resist a daughter's sweet plea? "I'd love to."

"Do you think Terry will be set for the day?" Jacob lifted a brow in question. "I don't want to push you into something you're not comfortable with, Josie."

She added kind and considerate about work-related stress to the already long list of reasons to like this man. "I'll double-check, but he should be fine. Nothing like being in the thick of things to get a handle on how stuff works. And I do tend to take over when I'm there, so this is probably a good thing." She made the call, decided everything was fine for a few more hours, then settled back into her seat as they drove north. And when they'd parked the car and crossed the narrow streets to the wide, spreading beach at Charlotte, Addie kicked off her shoes and spun in the sand. "This is huge, Dad! It's not like our lake at all."

"Last time I looked we didn't have a lake, Addie."

"You know the one I mean." She scolded him with the cutest face. "The one I love so much where I want to live forever and ever!"

He didn't sigh, but he looked like he wanted to, and Josie couldn't blame him. Addie wasn't afraid to stand her ground or make her wishes known, and there was no denying the sensibility of her choices. Why leave when you've found the perfect place? Except, of course, it wasn't perfect at all. Nothing about their current situation was ideal.

"Look that way!" Addie pointed north, across the huge lake. "You can't even see anything on the other side! How come it's so big?"

Jacob made a face, so Josie answered. "There are five huge lakes like this, Addie. The Great Lakes. And what you can't see across the water is Canada, another whole, huge country."

"Are you kidding me?" She whirled, delighted by this new fact. "We could be in another country if we swam over?"

"That would be some swim, kid, but if we were to take a boat over, we'd hit Canada. But it has to be a fairly big boat because I expect these big lakes can get rocking."

"They sure do."

"Can I dig in the sand? Please?"

"Absolutely, except we didn't exactly come prepared." Jacob lifted his shoulders.

Josie spotted driftwood up the beach. "Nature provides." She pointed to the wood and headed that way. They traced roads into the sand with the sticks, and while they had no buckets to form castles, they mounded damp sand from below. Addie searched the beach for decorations. Shells, twigs, dried seaweed… And when they'd finished a fairly crude-looking castle, Jacob called her over, reached out his arm and took a selfie of all three of them.

A family photo.

Josie tried to push the thought aside, but that's what it felt like, sitting there with Jacob behind her, and Addie to her right, leaning into her sand-dusted arm.

Normally she hated the feel of sand in her clothes, and on her skin, but not today. Because today was all about Addie, and that made everything better.

"How about that carousel, kid?" Jacob pointed east. "It's pretty cool-looking."

"Yes, and I want to ride the wildest horse, the kind that go up and down, not the boring kind that just sit there. Okay, Dad?"

"The beach is pretty quiet today, so I think we can make that happen."

Young parents dotted the beach with little ones. What appeared to be preschool groups had been hosting picnics in the shaded park when they first arrived, but as the afternoon grew later, they'd packed up their things and headed home.

They walked through the park in the lull between little kids' awake time and high schoolers' streaming to the beach after school. Once they got to the carousel building, Addie adamantly refused to ride a horse, even a brightly painted one. "Dad. Josie!" She stood on the grass with them, waiting for the ride to slow down, but there was nothing slow about her enthusiasm as she watched. "Forget the horses, Dad, we can ride those anywhere. Do you see the rabbit?" She shrieked in excitement as the ride spun by. "And there's an ostrich or something like that, and there's a lion and a giraffe, and what are those, Dad?" She stepped closer until Jacob put a warning hand on her shoulder. "They're not horses, are they?"

"They're mules," Josie explained. "When my mom and dad brought us here, they were painted like zebras, but when the carousel went through a major overhaul, they realized the original artist had actually carved mules because mules helped build the Erie Canal. They're pretty cool, right?"

"So cool," Addie declared. "I want to ride a mule first, and then maybe the ostrich bird, and then maybe a lion, or a horse, or that huge rabbit! Is that okay, Dad?" She peeked up at him quickly. "Do we have enough money for that?"

"I really appreciate your asking. I think we're good," Jacob told her. "And you're right, we don't want to be greedy or expect too much."

"Because that would make God's heart sad." Addie shared a look with Jacob that said she understood. "I'll try not to be greedy, Dad, but

I love having fun!" She raced forward once the ride stopped, chose a mule, refused Jacob's help and climbed on.

"Here we go!"

When Jacob stayed there, she shooed him away from her side before the ride started. "Dad." She faced him at eye level, clearly taking charge. "Dads only ride with little kids who don't know to hang on. I'm six." Her frank expression said "I've got this," and Josie was happy to see Jacob back off.

"All right, then."

He stepped off and took a place at her side, watching, and when the back of his hand brushed hers, he folded her hand into his, nice and snug.

She should pull away.

She didn't. She glanced down, then up.

He was smiling, and he squeezed her hand lightly to let her know he caught the look, but kept his eyes on Addie. Then when the ride got started, he slanted a look her way. "My hand likes holding yours, Josie."

"Jacob."

"Shh." He pressed her hand lightly again. "I don't need reminders that this is all going to come to an end, but right now, it feels more right than anything's felt in a long time. Except for her." He dipped his head toward the carou-

sel and waved with his free hand when Addie
came around. "A guy. A girl. A cute kid and
a day at the beach. Sounds like a handholding
kind of moment to me. Wouldn't you agree?"

"If there's a custard sundae at the end of all
this, then I'm in." She kept it light, when the
last thing she wanted to do was keep it light.

"Is Abbott's as good as Stan's?" he asked,
and she winced on purpose.

"Better. But I won't ever tell Stan that, because he's a pillar of the community. But whenever I get up into the suburbs near Rochester,
I sneak over to Abbott's Frozen Custard. It's
a thing."

The carousel paused. Addie scrambled off
her mule and handed the ride operator more
tickets once she perched on the rabbit, a hare in
flight. She preened their way as parents moved
kids on and off the brightly lit musical ride.

Jacob gently squeezed Josie's hand again.
When she looked up, he wasn't watching Addie.

He was watching her.

Her eyes. Her face. Her mouth. His gaze lin-
gered there, and as the ride swept Addie away,
he leaned down and touched his lips to hers, a
feather-light kiss, just enough to make her wish
for another. And then another, yet.

She started to protest, but when he kissed
her the second time, she didn't want to protest.

She wanted to melt, and maybe she did melt, just a little.

He pulled back and smiled. "I couldn't stop wondering, Josie. And couldn't stop thinking about it." He waved as Addie went by, then winked at Josie.

"And now?"

"I still won't be able to stop thinking about it," he mused, still smiling. "But for very different reasons."

"Jacob…"

"I know. I know why it can't possibly work because my job's about to take me to the other end of the country."

He didn't know all the reasons. He didn't know the most important one of all, the one that would make him see her quite differently.

She wanted to tell him. She wanted to clear the air, once and for all. A bright summer's day was a perfect opening for that, but when she opened her mouth, he shushed her with one finger. "We don't have to talk it to death right now, do we? Unless you have a major objection, let's just enjoy the day. And then later we can fret over all the things grown-ups fret about. Right now, let's just have fun with her. All right?"

She should press, because she knew the secret she held, but she acquiesced.

He was right. There would be fussing and

fuming soon enough. For today, things were practically perfect, and she was going to allow herself to enjoy the moment. When regret came later, as she knew it would, she'd have this day to look back on and no one could ever take that away from her.

"I can't wait to tell Memaw and Pawpaw about my great adventures!" Addie wriggled in the backseat as Jacob pulled the car into the employee parking behind the hotel. "Do you think Memaw is feeling better?"

"She texted me that she was, but that she was going to bed early tonight and she'll hear about your day tomorrow."

"Do I have to go to school tomorrow, Dad? For real?"

He stood firm deliberately. Ginger had finagled her way around their parents with such finesse, it became impossible to stop when she grew older. He wasn't going to tip Addie in a similar direction. "Yup. And the next day. And then you're done for summer, so let's not argue about it."

"But—"

"Adeline Rose."

"Humph." She slumped back into her seat, arms crossed. "We're not doing anything in school, so

I don't know why I should go when Memaw and Pawpaw want to spend time with me."

"Fortunately, your grandparents also put great value on a solid education."

"It's hard to let go of a fun day, isn't it?" Josie's soft-spoken empathy lightened the moment.

Addie bobbed her head. "I just want it to keep going forever."

"But you know what would happen if it did?" Josie asked in the same quiet tone.

Addie shook her head.

"You'd get bored. Special never seems as special once it becomes everyday ordinary, and you'd wish for something else."

Addie frowned, unconvinced. "I don't think that would happen."

"Well, what's your favorite food at Christmas?"

"Pawpaw's apple pancakes!"

"And do you think they'd taste as special at Christmas if you had them every single day?"

Addie's frown softened. "Like maybe I'd get tired of them?"

"Like that, yes."

"I don't know if I would," Addie told her, then tried and failed to stifle a monster-size yawn. "But maybe it wouldn't be so wonderful if you get it all the time."

"A lesson learned."

"But I wouldn't mind trying to see!"

Jacob laughed as Josie climbed out of the car on one side and he did the same on the other. "I expect you're going into the restaurant to check things out."

"I'll finish the evening shift here, head home, and then we hit the ground running for the next couple of weeks. Are you ready for this grand opening, Jacob?"

He'd come around the front of the car as she spoke. Now he faced her, wishing the day didn't have to come to an end, much like his daughter. "I'm ready. This is ready." He indicated the beautiful resort with a thrust of his head. "But I'm not ready for what comes later. The leaving part. And I'm not sure what to do about that, Josie."

She appeared to remain casual, but not before he spotted that now-familiar flash of regret. "Resign yourself because time has a way of marching on." She moved back slightly. "And shouldn't you have your résumés out there if you're parting ways with Carrington?"

"They're out there. I'm just not certain I want to be out there with them. But you're right, I've got to get her home to bed and tomorrow's going to come early. Mom and Dad are taking over with Addie for the next two weeks because

I know I'll be listed as unavailable while we get things ironed out here. And then—"

"Another chapter unfolds." She leaned down and waved to Addie in the backseat. "See you later, sweet thing! Thanks for letting me tag along today!"

"Bye, Josie! Thank you!"

She didn't turn back his way. She didn't pause to flirt. True to her word, she kept a distance he wished he could broach, but unless he was willing to take a whole new turn in life, she was right to walk away.

She disappeared into the Bayou Barbecue through the back entrance as Carly Moore, one of the young and very good-looking IT managers came his way. Carly's swagger and short skirt said she wasn't afraid to draw attention to herself, even in the workplace. "Jacob, got a quick minute to touch base on a few things?"

"Just that long," he replied. "Addie's with me and I need to get her home."

Carly waved to Addie in the backseat before she began. "I wanted to let you know we should have everything running seamlessly on the security end and the Wi-Fi capabilities. The team and I have gone through the exercises, and it all looks good, but I'll be on hand opening week in case we hit a glitch. Something about a thousand people using hundreds of devices simultaneously can mess things up. Was that Josie Gallagher you were with?"

She sounded surprised, as if seeing him with Josie was unlikely, and that put an instant burr between his shoulder blades. "It was. Why?"

"No reason." She rolled one very shapely shoulder. "I just never figured you for the wild-child type. Of course, she's calmed down now, I'm sure, but in our college days at Fredonia, we're talking one busy, busy girl. If you get my drift."

He got her drift all right, and wanted to leap to Josie's defense, then realized he could do that—and end up looking downright stupid because he had no idea what Josie was like a dozen years back.

Did he care?

He climbed into the car, thinking.

No, not really. A lot of kids made stupid college mistakes, including him. But the words stuck in his craw...*wild child*.

The thought of the strong, sensitive woman he was getting to know being a wild child seemed impossible on some levels, and not so much on others.

She did her own thing. He liked that about her.

She had a mind of her own, and stepped outside the norm. She'd built a great business on the premise of hard work and sacrifice, with no big Wharton degrees next to her name.

Wild child.

The brand irked him. Partially because of what it intimated, and partly—if he was honest with himself—because he was afraid it might be true.

He got Addie home, showered and tucked into bed long before the late-June sun went down, and when she was asleep, his hand reached for the phone. He had people he could call. People who could check Josie out. Within a day, he'd know enough, but as his fingers brushed the phone, he pulled his hand away.

He was thirty-six. She was in her early thirties. What did it matter if she'd messed up in college over a decade before?

He wasn't interested in the college-age Josie. He was falling for the woman he saw now— the beautiful, kind and faith-filled woman who seemed perfect with Addie, and maybe—just maybe—perfect for him.

He left the phone alone, took his own shower and went to bed.

Carly Moore was a top-notch IT person in the Central New York area. The team she brought on board planned their work and worked their plan, top flight.

But he didn't need her snippy innuendo or

rolled shoulders to influence his choices. And unless he flipped his life upside down, his choices lay many miles south.

But when he closed his eyes, it wasn't job opportunities that crossed his mind as it used to be. It was a hazel-eyed, tawny-skinned woman with long, thick, dark hair. A woman who seemed at peace with God, his daughter and running a top-notch business. A woman with enough strength to be admired, and enough warmth to draw him closer.

"As the lily among thorns, so is my love among the daughters." The quote from the Song of Solomon tweaked him.

Josie never spoke ill of others. She worked quietly and carefully, with a winning nature, but stood strong when things hadn't gone her way.

Wild child...

The phrase irritated him, but what irked him more was that now that it had been spoken, he couldn't get it out of his head, and that was the biggest bother of all.

Chapter Eleven

Josie saw the unfamiliar number in her phone and answered the call as she double-checked the smoker on grand opening morning.

Excitement warred with nerves, and she was happy to be behind the scenes, controlling what she did best, the flow of great food at reasonable prices. She'd never planned on being part of a larger whole; she'd been fine on her own. But that all changed last winter, and here she was, part of the grand resort, a new beginning. "Josie Gallagher speaking."

"Miss Gallagher, this is Keshia Holmes from Sweet Hope Adoptions in Greenville."

No.

She couldn't do this now. She couldn't reasonably listen to what Ms. Holmes had to say in the middle of opening-day crazy. "Ms. Holmes, this isn't a good time. I'm at work and there's no time to go into this right now."

"I assumed that, because you haven't returned my calls or answered the phone when I used a marked agency phone."

"Ms. Holmes—"

"I understand this is hard," the woman pressed on. "The entire agency understands the difficulty in this most unfortunate turn of events, and we want you to know that while we assume no responsibility for the dishonest actions of others, we realize this situation has created an unforeseen predicament."

Unforeseen? Did she really just say that?

Josie's pulse sped up. "What you're calling unforeseen was seen clearly by others. Relatives and friends. So I'm not sure your choice of words is accurate, Ms. Holmes."

"Of course the home study was done to our usual thorough standards, as was the county home study," the woman continued.

Rule number one: Don't throw bad facts at a really mad mama. "Brewer County's human services has been complaining about being underfunded and understaffed for a decade, and those are only the formal complaints I've been able to find online, so I don't think your argument about the home study will prove satisfactory. It clearly wasn't done well enough, and I'd have more respect for you if you simply admitted that. When the people in charge are willing to brush off ineptitude and/or misconduct, how can your clients have faith in the system? I put my trust in you to screen potential parents properly. Now I'm wondering if you didn't just put out feelers for a socially acceptable appearance or for a couple who was willing to pay the highest price."

"Miss Gallagher, I assure you, that wasn't the case and I've gone through the files personally."

Josie wanted to scream.

She didn't. She took a breath, thought about what Cruz had told her, and changed her tone. "Ms. Holmes, here's the situation as I see it. Your agency didn't do the job to the best of its ability. You can contest that, you can argue the point, but from our end, that's a fact. You allowed a fraudulent couple to sneak through the system. Having said that, during our current conversation you've referred to this matter as a situation and a predicament."

Josie paused to take a deep breath. "It is neither," she continued. "It is a precious child put into a situation that left her with no father, and an adoptive mother to pick up the pieces. An adoptive mother who kept up the charade of having a husband on hand while my daughter and I were undergoing liver transplants. Which means she didn't want me investigating further all those years ago."

Josie took another deep breath. She wanted to punch someone. She wanted to go toe-to-toe with this woman and let her know how this whole thing felt from the birth mother's perspective. That being lied to over something as perfectly wonderful as a child went way beyond a margin of error.

It was a dagger, straight to the heart, because the one thing she'd tried to do right in the face of a grievous wrong was to ensure Addie's place in a strong, nuclear family. "You've spoken with my lawyer. And I'm sure you're busily assembling a legal team to ward off any bad publicity, but the first step is to admit you made a mistake. For the sake of children and mothers everywhere, I pray to God you can, at some point, manage at least that."

Shaken, she disconnected the call.

She'd avoided the agency calls for the last several days on purpose because how was she supposed to concentrate on the massive job ahead of her, Addie and Jacob's upcoming move and the waves of emotions sweeping over her daily?

Addie's placement wasn't a predicament, and the child herself wasn't a situation. She was a gift from God, and Sweet Hope hadn't taken that as seriously as they should have.

She needed to talk to her family, but there was no time for that today.

And she needed to tell Jacob, straight out, but for the upcoming weekend, there would be no time to talk, and barely time to breathe.

He'd hate her.

Ginger's parents would hate her.

And Addie…

She firmed her jaw, having made her decision.

Addie would never know because she had no intention of telling her. This wasn't Addie's fault, and she shouldn't bear fallout from the actions of foolish adults.

Once again she would put Addie first. She had to tell Jacob, especially if the adoption agency was examining records. After messing up the first time around, she was certain they'd be more careful now. Better he hear it from her than them.

But then the Weatherlys would leave, Josie would stay and Addie would have the sweet, normal life her mother had promised her in utero.

Her chest tightened as she choked back emotion. It put a vise grip on her aching heart, but she'd gone through heartache before and mustered up. She'd do the same now, because Addie was worth the sacrifice. But in the background she wanted that agency to take responsibility for its error because surrendering a child wasn't a casual affair. Following through on the proper home vetting the agency professionals promised birth mothers shouldn't be casual, either.

"Are you ready for the big day?"

Jacob. Here. Now.

She swiped a hand to her face, but there was no way to hide the tears.

"Josie, hey." He crossed the short space between them in an instant and drew her into his arms. "Hey, hey, it's all right. I know it's crazy, but it will be fine, I promise. I've been through lots of these, and we haven't lost a chef yet."

He thought she was suffering an attack of nerves because of the grand opening, and he wanted to comfort her. Hold her. How she wished she could stay right there, in the circle of this good man's arms and just be herself.

She couldn't. And when he learned the truth, he wouldn't be offering any more of those kind, loving hugs.

She stepped back.

He offered her a hanky from his suit pocket, but she refused it and used a scrub cloth instead. "I am not getting your clean pocket square messy two hours before we officially open the doors." She tossed the dirty cloth into the laundry tote inside the kitchen and grabbed tissues. "I'm fine, just a little overwhelmed for the moment. But with so much to do, it will be fine. Just fine."

"It will." He set his hands on her shoulders and smiled, but the smile didn't quite erase the concern in his eyes. "When things settle down, I'd like to have time to just sit and talk together. Wouldn't that be nice, Josie? Just you and me and some good coffee? Away from all of this?"

It didn't just sound nice.

It sounded amazing. But it wouldn't happen because it couldn't happen once he knew the truth. "It sounds marvelous, but right now I've got to get my head back in the game. With coffee." She popped a pod into her brewing system and grabbed cream and sugar. "And please, don't let this worry you." She waved toward the smoker area, where he'd surprised her. "I'm fine and the restaurant will be fine."

"I wasn't worried about that. I know you've got it covered." He touched her cheek with his right hand, a whisper of a touch, calming. Soothing. "I was just worried about you."

His eyes, so blue, a shade that darkened when he worried and brightened in the sun. His hair, a fresh trim for opening day, crisp and sharp. Today he'd stand with other prominent figures, movers and shakers from Carrington Hotels and town officials, with all the pomp and circumstance of a multimillion-dollar endeavor being successfully launched on the Eastern shore...

He belonged there, among the more gilded.

She didn't.

Oh, she didn't hate herself for her earlier mistakes. God had forgiven her, and she'd forgiven herself, but she'd learned something about Josie Gallagher in the ensuing years.

She wasn't a front-door person. She was a back-door gal, the kind of woman who did well out of the limelight. The kitchen suited her. So did the casual "dive" appeal they'd layered into the Bayou decor. It fit.

And when she saw Jacob in the grand lobby two hours later, surrounded by all kinds of designer suits, made for the occasion, and his parents right there, with Addie, dressed in a simple and quite expensive sailor girl outfit...

She saw how well they all fit together.

She was the outsider, first by choice, now by timing, but as long as Addie was beloved and happy, Josie could live with that.

Cruz leaned forward as Kate Gallagher set down a pitcher of sweet tea and several glasses the following evening. "Time's running out, Josie."

The ticking of Aunt Kate's mantel clock added weight to his words. She looked at her mother, then Kimberly and Aunt Kate and sighed.

He tapped the folder in front of him. "If the agency is calling you, they're likely to have their lawyer get a hold of Jacob soon, once they feel like they've got a solid argument on their side. Although he's an innocent party, the agency's legal team would be foolish not to bring him on board, and that could happen at any moment."

That had been her worry from the moment she saw the agency name on her phone display. "I realized that when they first called me on Thursday, but I figured I'd have through the weekend. I'll tell him on Monday, Cruz."

Cruz grimaced instantly, but Josie raised a hand to halt his argument. "It's crazy at the resort right now. His time is winding down, and he'll be moving on to the next job. And once he knows I'm not going to try and regain custody—"

"Are you sure about that, Josie?" Cissy slipped an arm around Josie's shoulders. "Because if you do, you know we'll support you, one hundred percent."

She shifted her attention to her mother. "I'd love the chance to be her mother, but I can't do that to her. She's happy and stable, and Jacob is, well—" She raised her shoulders in a shrug as Kimberly patted baby Elizabeth's back for a burp. "He's wonderful. He's a good, kind man and he wants what's best for Addie. I can't disrupt the peaceful life she has. I know I set certain parameters for her adoption. I really wanted a two-parent family because it's good for kids to have a mom and a dad. But Jacob is marvelous with her, even though it can't be easy being a single parent. How could I live with myself if I were to selfishly wrench her away from the joy she's already only known for such a short time?"

"You've got courage, kid. I'm not offering advice one way or another," Kimberly told her, "but I can't imagine how hard this has been. Still, I believe you're doing the right thing, and maybe once the agency realizes that, they'll back off."

"But if they think I won't press, they might not put better safeguards in place," Josie explained. "If I back off now, they skate free and maybe they improve, maybe they don't. But if they're scared of being called out—"

"Which they should be!" declared Cissy.

Josie hugged her mother's arm. "Then maybe

we can make some good out of all this. My schedule is packed full for tomorrow. Come Monday, I'll face the music."

"Do you want me there, darling?" Cissy leaned her head against Josie's. "I'll happily stand by your side."

"Great." Josie angled a doubtful look her way. "Then you'll cry and I'll cry and we'll have a total mess on our hands." She hugged her mother but shook her head. "I'm doing this one alone. Face-to-face, the way I should have done when Addie came strolling out of that car."

"You didn't know where you stood or what kind of man Jacob was back then," Drew reminded her as he took the baby from his wife. "Now we know. Now we move forward."

"Thank you." Josie stood. She'd staved off tears because she'd shed far too many of them the past few weeks.

She wasn't a crier in general, but seeing Addie, getting to know Jacob and realizing what she could have gained if things had been different…

But things weren't different, and that was the truth of the matter. "Thanks, guys. I appreciate all the love and the support and the legal stuff you've done for me."

"We've got your back, Josie." Drew kissed

his baby Elizabeth's forehead as he paced the floor, hoping to ease her belly discomfort. "Always."

"I know that now." She raised her shoulders and sighed. "And I should have known back then. So..." She moved toward the door and raised a hand. "I'll let you guys know how things go on Monday, all right?"

"Yes. Are you coming to church with us in the morning?" her mother asked. Her mother and two aunts on the Morgan side of the family attended the same church service every week, without fail. Josie caught church when she could, where she could, but for this week, she thought it might be real nice to sit in the pew with her mother. "Yes. I'll come straight from work, and head straight back. See you then."

"Okay."

She didn't go right back to the carriage house apartment she was renting from her aunt and uncle. She walked toward the beach instead, letting her thoughts take hold.

No matter what happened on Monday, she would tell Jacob the truth, the whole truth.

And then she'd walk away, at least as far as she could with a major responsibility under the Eastern Shore roof.

His time in Grace Haven was drawing to a close. She could stay out of his way, and out of Addie's life, for those last few days. She'd hate it, but she'd do it because it was the right thing to do.

"Addie has fallen in love with this place," Bob Weatherly noted on Saturday night.

"She reminds me of that on a regular basis," Jacob replied. "What she doesn't know is that I've gotten two firm offers, one in Austin and one outside of Knoxville, Tennessee. And they're both companies where I can hang my hat for the duration."

"Which is how long?"

"However long it takes to raise a little girl on my own," Jacob said softly. "I want her to feel like she's part of a community. A school, a church, a neighborhood. The chance to play soccer or baseball or any of the things kids do when they're being raised in a normal American setting. Carrington is offering me a whole lot of money to stay on for the Outer Banks proposal, but then we'd be done in eighteen months and moving again. I want more for her than that."

"She hasn't suffered from your work," his father noted. "She's about the best-adjusted kid I've ever met."

"Exactly why I need to do this now," Jacob acknowledged, "to help her stay that way. It was okay to bounce around for preschools, but now she needs something more solid and stable."

"Have you considered Florida?" his mother asked while Addie finished decorating a fairly complicated coloring page for a six-year-old in the cool breeze of the lakeside porch.

"My recruiter looked around, but there wasn't anything that appealed to me. And frankly, Mom, I know you like it, but that hot and humid air is tough on me and the kid." He smiled in Addie's direction. "Texas is probably out because of that, too, even though it's a drier heat. And Knoxville?" He made a face. "I wanted to stay close enough to you guys that we can visit regularly. And I'm still waiting to hear on a probable offer outside of Raleigh. I think we could both handle North Carolina, and maybe Addie would reclaim her drawl."

His mother arched a brow in mock disapproval. "She sounds like a Yankee, Jacob. There's precious little Southern in her now. I had to instruct her how to draw out her words, proper-like."

Sheila spoke up so Addie would hear that last part. Addie laughed at her table. So did Jacob. "She picked up the Yankee twang real quick, that's for certain. Either way, I'll make a decision in the next week or so. And we'll move on."

"Except only one of us wants to move on." Addie didn't get up, but she aimed a look his way. "One of us really likes this town, Daddy. I don't see why we don't at least look for a job here. We're both happy in this place and that should be the most important thing of all."

"Have you looked, son?" Bob kept his voice soft so Addie wouldn't hear.

"I did, and there's not a lot up here right now. There's expansion over in Victor. It's a pretty town that's become a shopping hub, and in some of the eastside towns surrounding Rochester, but nothing that needs a major player on board. Addie—" he stood and tapped his watch "—we've got to head home. There's church in the morning."

"Which one?"

"I thought we'd go to the Grace Haven Community tomorrow. We haven't been to that one in a while."

"I love those big, pretty windows!" Addie tucked the crayons into their sack and set them on top of the coloring books. "Do you guys want to come with us?" She crossed the room and grabbed her grandparents' hands. "It would be really special if you do."

Would his parents meet them at church for

Addie? They'd fallen out of the church habit when Jacob was a boy and weekend life got crazy busy.

"Not this time, dear." His mother patted Addie's cheek but didn't cave, even when Addie offered her best and brightest smile. "We'll see you afterward and maybe we can go to breakfast together while Daddy works. You'd like that, wouldn't you?"

Addie hugged his mother. "I always like to be with you, Memaw. Before church or after church or during church, I just always love to be near you guys."

His mother's eyes filled. She hugged Addie, then moved to the kitchen of the lake house, pretending there was something to do. "We'll see you both in the morning, then?"

"Sounds good." He got Addie back to the apartment and tucked into bed as the sun sank low on the western horizon.

He didn't want to think about leaving. He'd realized that on Thursday, when he found Josie upset.

He didn't want to walk away from her.

Was he being silly or shortsighted? He didn't think so, but he couldn't stay up north when the job offers were coming in down south.

Or could he? Could he trust in God enough to believe things would work out?

He winced because he knew the answer to that question. He didn't do chancy things because he didn't like risk, especially where Addie was concerned. A good job, a normal home, a solid life: he owed her that much.

As he was thinking that, his recruiter messaged him a bite—a good bite—a job offer with a large-scale local developer.

He drew up the offer on his laptop and studied it.

It was a substantial chance, and the opportunity to stay here in Central New York.

I'll look this over, but I'm interested, he messaged back. Definitely interested.

He hit Send and went to bed reconsidering his choices.

It wasn't close to his parents. That was a drawback. But the airport was only thirty minutes west, and they could get flights to Florida for key vacation weeks. It wasn't perfect. He knew that. But to stay here, to have the opportunity to get to know Josie better, and maybe even make some serious changes in his life?

Yeah.

He smiled as he settled into his pillow.

He could definitely live with that.

Chapter Twelve

"Dad! I see Josie over there!" Addie grabbed his arm and pointed to the right side of the small stone church. "Can we sit with her? Please?"

"Sure."

He waited as Addie slid into the pew, then followed.

She hugged Josie, then reached around and hugged Josie's mother, too. "Good morning, Mrs. Gallagher." She hissed the whisper that wasn't all that much of a whisper.

"Addie. Good morning, darling girl." Josie's mother smiled wide and noted Addie's outfit. "I love your dress. And those sandals are very popular right now."

"Thank you!" Addie preened, then leaned into Josie's arm as if meant to be there. "I'm so excited we get to sit together in church! Dad and I like to go to different churches, to see what's going on."

"Plus my daughter likes to meet new people," Jacob added softly.

"I do that, too." Josie patted Addie's arm. "I like hearing the different preachers and appreciating the different settings."

"Dad, see what I mean? Josie likes the same things we do. I think that's really, really nice, don't you?"

He did think it was nice, and when Josie lifted those hazel eyes to his, he was pretty sure doing anything with Josie Gallagher would be the nicest thing of all. "I concur. But, shh." He indicated the organist with a glance. "Time to pay attention."

When the service ended, Jacob waited a few moments for Addie to light a candle.

She loved lighting candles in churches; it had become a thing with her when they'd moved here. She'd make a donation, light a candle, then kneel and say a prayer. To Addie, it didn't matter what kind of church she was in. If it had a bank of votives, she made sure to light one.

When they stepped outside a few minutes later, it took a moment for his eyes to adjust to the bright, sunlit day. When they did, he looked around.

No Josie.

Her mother was standing at the edge of the walkway, though, with two women. One of the women poked Cissy Gallagher and pointed to Addie. "Cissy, that little one looks enough like you to be your twin when you were that age. Do you see that, Jillian? Same hair, same eyes."

"You're being silly," Cissy told her as Jacob and Addie drew closer, but not in a normal mode of speech. She looked nervous, as if the other woman's words meant something.

"I expect it's the accidents of color, but Audrey's right." The third woman smiled their way. "She looks way more like you than any of your children did."

"And I expect Addie is complimented by the thought of looking like you, Mrs. Gallagher." Jacob palmed Addie's head. "I have to admit, I think she's pretty darned cute myself."

"Oh, she is." The third woman offered her hand. "I'm Cissy's sister, Jillian. And I want to congratulate you on the success of your opening. We're quite excited about the opportunities the Eastern Shore Inn will afford to folks around here. A job well done."

"Thank you." He turned toward Josie's mother. "Did Josie head back to work?"

"Yes." She gazed up at him with a frank look, as if she wanted to say more, but didn't. "A busy day, she said."

"Our first Sunday, so yes. I expect it will be cranking. Ladies, a pleasure meeting you." He tucked Addie's hand in his and moved on.

Folks waved to him as he passed. The pastor stopped him and they chatted briefly. Around him, summer flowers bloomed, boughs of thick, green leaves offered welcome shade, and a sky so blue it seemed unreal provided the perfect backdrop.

He could live here, he realized.

He could make this their home, and maybe, if things went right, it wouldn't be just a home for him and Addie.

The thought of a home with Josie made him walk faster. He dropped Addie off at his parents' rental cottage and headed to the resort.

People milled about the beach.

Bright umbrellas dotted the sandy shore, and folks were docking boats where Josie's restaurant used to be, a few hundred feet up the shore.

Kids ran in the sand, and there were two lifeguards stationed on either side of the beach, a picturesque summer scene.

As he slipped into the office wing through a side door, he thought about his choices and a new to-do list.

Take the job here in Central New York. Buy a house. Get him and Addie moved in before school started. Court the girl he couldn't stop thinking about.

He grinned.

He had a good offer on the table. If it wasn't perfect, he could look for other options, but it was a start and it bought him time. He had a decent bank account balance and the luxury of time, at least a summer's worth. He'd take the job, stay right here and woo the fair lady.

Josie was contracted. She wasn't going anywhere.

He had every choice in the world, but whenever he pictured that gorgeous long hair and those luminescent eyes, the choices narrowed to here. Right here.

The day raced by. He had a few small fires to put out, unforeseen systems snags, but by the end of the day, nothing major had occurred and the online reviews of the Eastern Shore Inn were stellar. Those solid reviews would keep the entire Carrington business machine happy.

Josie went to work on Monday, fairly sure her heart might not make it through the day.

Jacob was nowhere to be found, which made sense because he'd been working long, rugged hours, just like her.

Should she make an appointment to see him? Stop into his office? Text him?

She decided the text was easiest and least volatile. Can we meet later today for that talk?

Short and sweet, following up on his suggestion. His text came back quickly. Yes. This afternoon, after four? Coffee someplace quiet?

She'd love that, but she couldn't risk telling him the truth in a public place. Plus, any place quiet probably wouldn't stay quiet for long after what she had to tell him. Too many people. My apartment? Five o'clock?

In that case, I'll bring the coffee.

Kind and considerate. And sure to dislike her by the end of the day. Great. See you then.

She put away the phone and layered the smoker while the kitchen staff worked with yesterday's meat selection. They'd prepped the soups, and already the restaurant was filled with the enticing scents of good, solid food.

Gabby Gallagher's bakery supplied her with homemade pies and hummingbird cake each day. Her signature French toast and bread puddings filled out the dessert menu, along with the ever-popular crème brûlée.

And Robert Weatherly had raved about her barbecue at first bite.

He wouldn't be raving once the truth was known, but she couldn't help that.

She prayed.

She prayed for courage as she tended the smoker, for strength as she oversaw the making of salads and, as she grated robust Vermont cheddar for the Cajun rice and broccoli, mostly she prayed for understanding.

The last one was the least likely. Josie knew that, because she didn't pretend to understand any of this. Right now it wasn't about blame. There was plenty of that to go around.

It was about love, and if you loved something enough, you set it free. And that's what she had to do later this afternoon.

Jacob spotted the unfamiliar Georgia number and took the call on his Bluetooth as he drove toward the resort. "Jacob Weatherly, Carrington Hotels, how can I help you?"

"Mr. Weatherly, I'm James Sinclair of Sinclair Associates in Atlanta. We represent Sweet Hope Adoption Agency."

Sweet Hope Adoption? Jacob's interest switched to high gear. "The adoption agency that handled my daughter's original adoption to my sister."

"And her husband."

Jacob let that slide because he knew—they all knew—that Adam had no intention of staying in his marriage to Ginger. It had been the talk of the family for months. But that was neither here nor there now. "Have you uncovered something in Addie's family history, some medical thing? Why are you calling?"

"No, there is no bad medical news to report, and that's a wonderful thing, isn't it?"

Jacob was losing his patience and his focus. He pulled off onto one of the graveled overlooks because a conversation with a lawyer about Addie hadn't made his list of probabilities that day. "Mr. Sinclair, what's going on? Why the phone call? What's happened?"

"Adeline's birth mother has hired an attorney."

His heart didn't pause. It stopped. "She *what*?"

"In fact, she hired a highly regarded Manhattan attorney who has been looking into the incidentals of Adeline's adoption."

His phrasing irritated Jacob further, which is why Carrington tended to put him on diplomatic issues in place of their legal team. Most lawyers didn't do diplomacy well. "There are no incidentals in adoption. It's a straightforward process, bound by courts. For goodness' sake, Addie is six years old!" He raked a hand through his short hair. "Why would her mother come looking for her now?"

"Questions have been raised about the original home studies."

That made no sense, none whatsoever. "They had a lovely home. I don't understand."

"The lawyer is contesting that your brother-in-law was not invested in the marriage."

That was certainly true enough. "He wasn't. He hadn't been in some time, and we all wondered why my sister thought it was a good time to adopt a child, but she'd miscarried several times and we knew how much she wanted to be a mother. And she was a good mother."

"Mr. Weatherly, technically I'm not advising you to keep that information to yourself, but insinuating that the poor condition of your sister's marriage was widespread knowledge could be detrimental to our cause."

"Our cause?" The collar of his shirt rose slightly. The palms of his hands went damp. "What is our cause?"

"To hopefully offer this woman a satisfactory settlement and tuck this inquiry quietly away."

"Buy her off?" Anger didn't simply roll up his spine, it raced. "The agency is thinking of buying off a drug-using mother because she brings some lame claim six years later? I—" He couldn't have this conversation sitting in the car. He climbed out, took the phone and began pacing. "This is preposterous."

"I wish it were, but it is not, Mr. Weatherly. Adeline's specific adoption had a clause written in at the request of the birth mother. Sweet Hope pledged to honor that clause and offer only happily married couples as options. Your sister's portfolio portrayed a loving couple in a barren state, offering all kinds of enticements for the betterment of the child."

"And money? Money for the birth mother? Does it mention that?" He spat out the words. Ginger had procured a substantial sum from his parents to cover the birth mother's medical costs, and they'd given it willingly.

The attorney hesitated. He could hear the man breathing on the other end of the phone, and the soft rustle of papers moving. Then he spoke again, and his careful words sent Jacob's heart into a kind of free fall. "The birth mother accepted no money from anyone in this adoption, Mr. Weatherly. I'm not sure where you got that information, but there was no exchange of funds. She had medical insurance and self-funded her prenatal care. Your sister did pay the stated agency fees that covered standard administrative expenses."

No payout?

He ran his brain around that quickly, because he was sure Ginger had referenced that. And it made her decision to name him as guardian harder, because his parents had handed over nearly thirty thousand dollars to ensure Addie's adoption. Who'd have thought then that he needed to recall details of the adoption six years later? "Walk me back, here. You said the birth mother contacted you now."

"A lawyer representing her interests contacted the agency for protocol and ran an independent investigation into the legality of the original adoption. And that's why I'm calling you."

Legality of the original adoption?

Jacob had been around legal beagles long enough to understand the nuances of a contract. If the original contract was not binding, then follow-up contracts could be declared null and void. "Are you telling me that my adoption of Addie might not hold up in court?"

He couldn't swallow.

He could barely breathe.

The bright July sun disappeared from the sky, and the warm summer air seemed cold—suddenly very cold. Or was that just the chills running up and down his spine?

"We don't want this to go to court, Mr. Weatherly." The firm tenor of the other man's voice indicated that court wouldn't be a good idea. "We want to settle out of court at the agency's full expense, of course. They keep insurance for these sorts of things."

"These sorts of things?" Had he just heard

the man correctly? Was he implying that mistakes in adoptions weren't a major exception? And that an error in judgment six years ago could mess up a child's life now? "This can't be happening. No, wait, let me rephrase that. This will not happen. The day I took that little girl into my care I promised her and God that I would do everything in my power to give her the life she finally deserved. Free from cancer, free from grief and sorrow, to the best of my ability. Her birth mother can't simply waltz in, six years later, and declare herself wronged. There must be a statute of limitations in effect. This can't possibly be legal."

"There is a statute, of course. But this goes beyond criminal proceedings—"

Criminal proceedings?

"And straight to a civil suit that could cite the agency and your late sister and her former husband with fraud. And because that was only discovered recently, the statute of limitations isn't called into play."

A lawsuit against his deceased sister. A lawsuit that could twist Addie's sweet life into a pretzeled mess. "No."

"Mr. Weatherly—"

"How did she get this information? How did this woman, with her scandalous past, ferret out information about my sister, her husband

and Addie? Something had to set this into motion, Mr. Sinclair. People don't just wake up one day and say, 'Oh, I think I'm going to look into something that happened six years before.' Do they?"

A long stretch of silence marked the other end of the phone. And then James Sinclair said words that made both no sense and absolute sense, all at once. "She saw you there, in Grace Haven. With her daughter. And she wanted to know what happened to Ginger and Adam O'Neill."

She saw him here? In Grace Haven?

His mind raced, and it raced in multiple directions, but he knew... He knew right off, because he'd seen the look on Josie's face. He hadn't understood it, but he'd seen it, and Addie had noticed it, too.

The hidden sadness. The sudden turnaround to take the Carrington lease offer. The kindnesses to Addie. The resemblance to Cissy Gallagher...

They'd known.

They'd known all this time and they'd played him like a fine-tuned Southern fiddle, weaving their ways around him, weaseling into his life. Into Addie's life.

Josie.

Wild child.

That's what Carly Moore had called her, and he could see it now, plain as day.

He wanted to throw up. He wanted this phone call to end. No, wait—he wanted it to never have occurred, because she'd not only fooled him, she'd made him care about her, care so much that he'd stupidly considered changing his life to suit hers. To woo her. To be part of her life.

His gut gripped tight. His hand shook.

She wanted to talk to him this afternoon, but that wasn't going to happen. Josie Gallagher and her little scheme to win the heart of an innocent child, then wrench her from the only home she'd known for years, wasn't going to get the respite of meeting on her terms.

"This is a lot to digest, Mr. Sinclair."

"I understand, and we deeply regret that, Mr. Weatherly. Of course, we don't want you to approach the birth mother. We need to keep the lines cleanly drawn for legal purposes."

Not approach her? He almost snorted. "So she can launch an investigation but I can't talk to her about it? I'm assuming we're talking about Josie Gallagher, correct?"

Mr. Sinclair refused to confirm the name, but that was all right. He didn't need to. "We'll simply refer to her as the birth mother at this point until a suit is officially filed. And I caution you, Mr. Weatherly, not to do anything that would negatively affect your standing as Addie's guardian."

"Father." Firm and cold, he let the solicitor know that his role wasn't and would never be reduced to that of a simple guardian. "I am her father. And don't you forget it."

"Of course, of course. A bad choice of words on my part, and a reality we'd like to help you maintain."

He couldn't mean that like it sounded. That somehow, someway, Josie could take Addie away from him. Who would do that? Who would tear a child apart like that for their own selfish gain?

Wild child...

The phrase gut-slammed him again.

Maybe he'd been stupid. Perhaps she'd fooled him completely, but it didn't matter. Nothing mattered except that she needed to know in no uncertain terms that Addie was his daughter. Random genetics didn't dictate a child's heritage. At some point, the basic science of the matter hit Pause and tender, loving care stepped in.

He hung up the call and didn't stop to pray or think or do any of those rational things he'd been taught as a major development negotiator.

He climbed behind the wheel, grabbed hold and drove toward the resort, fuming.

She thought she could upset Addie's life? She thought she could mess up the years he'd invested, giving his amazing daughter the faith, hope and love every child deserved?

She was wrong. And he was about to let her know it, and no amount of wringing hands and tears would make him see it any other way.

He knew.

The moment Josie turned from the walk-in cooler and saw Jacob standing inside the barbecue kitchen, she knew the hour had come.

"I need to see you outside."

The gruff tone of his voice made Terry turn, surprised. "Something wrong?"

Oh, there was something wrong, all right. Something so very wrong that words could never put it right. She saw that in Jacob's face, read it in his eyes. She slipped her apron off, left Terry to listen for timers and moved toward the door. "I'll be at the smoker, Terry."

"All right." He shot her a look as she glanced back, and she shook her head slightly. Terry was a good guy, and he was reacting to the cold steel in Jacob's voice, but this wasn't his fight. It wasn't supposed to be anyone's fight, but that had been taken out of her hands a long time ago.

She moved into the smoker "cave," turned and folded her hands across her middle. She gazed up at him, letting him take the lead.

"You're Addie's birth mother."

Oh, the cruel irony of words, the sharp-edged sword. How the sacrificial act of giving her child up had turned her into the bad guy here, she didn't know, but suddenly the words "birth mother" annoyed her. "I am her mother. Yes."

"Don't do that."

She waited, wishing this was over, wishing it had never gotten started. But then there would be no Addie, would there?

"Don't make the mere accident of genetics let you think you have rights, because you don't. You lied to me. You lied to my daughter. You lied to my parents, and to everyone around here, letting folks think you were an honorable person. All the while you were going behind my back, putting your tangled web of deceit into motion."

"I did nothing of the kind. Ever."

She hadn't thought he could look angrier. She was wrong. "You deny that you've got a lawyer looking into the original adoption? A closed adoption, according to the paperwork I was given, so how could you have known who Addie was unless you stalked her? Stalked them? What kind of person are you really, Josie? Because you fooled me." He crossed his arms, too. "And I didn't think I fooled easily. So shame on me for letting myself and my daughter get sucked into your ruse. But as of now, this moment, consider it over. My work is nearly complete here, and until it is, stay away from me, my family and especially my child. Do you hear me?"

Kind? Compassionate?

The man before her bore neither of those qualities, but she recognized his fear and pain because she'd lived it. "I'd already decided to have no further contact with Addie once you're gone."

He scoffed in disbelief. "Don't expect me to fall into line, Josie. To believe what you say now. Your actions speak louder than your words ever could. Just make sure you stay out of our sight. Out of our way. My daughter and I have no desire to further our acquaintance with a woman known around town as a 'wild child.'"

She could defend herself. She could cite all the things his sister had done to set up this confrontation, but what good would it do? She was stepping aside, a role she'd taken twice before. Addie was more important than her feelings and far more precious than her pride. "I'll stay out of your way. You stay out of mine."

He pulled back, surprised.

She waved a hand toward the restaurant. "My space. I'm working here, there's no reason for you to be here. Goodbye, Jacob."

She walked by him, into the restaurant and kept her head held high.

She would not lose it here, in public. She'd handled heartbreak before. Correction: she and God had handled it before. They'd do it again. Addie was safe, sound and, most of all, happy. She was beloved and treasured, and that's all Josie had ever wanted.

She didn't look back. She didn't care if Jacob went north or south around the complex, but she meant what she said. He had no further business being in her restaurant, her space. She'd declared it off-limits. She understood her choices better than anyone else. She'd made them long ago. But if he thought he could intimidate her or thrash her self-esteem any more than he already had?

He was wrong.

Chapter Thirteen

Sleep evaded him that night. When he showed up at his parents' cottage the next morning, concern darkened his father's gaze. "You look terrible."

"Jacob." His mother moved toward him while Addie gathered things from the backseat of the car. "Are you ill?"

"No, just a rough night. Not much sleep. Hey, listen, about this week—"

"I just paid the McCauleys another week's rent," his father cut in. "The people who'd booked had a sudden illness, and she was thrilled that we wanted to stay on. That will give us time with Addie while you look into this job arrangement you told us about."

"I never thought a child of mine would be comfortable living up north," Sheila added. "And yet, this place is so very charming, Jacob, and folks around here just love the way I talk. I do find their reactions positively refreshing!"

"I'm so glad Daddy is looking for a job up here!" Addie's excitement made his decision even harder to face. "It's like the best place ever, and maybe we can go shopping for a house and a cow!"

"Let's not rush things." He kept his voice calm on purpose, but while Addie seemed okay with his tone, his parents' expressions showed question. "You have fun with Memaw and Pawpaw today, and we'll figure things out later this week."

"Okay, Dad!" She hugged him, peppered his face with kisses when he leaned down, then slanted him a saucy look, half sweet, part sass. A look that had Josie Gallagher stamped all over it now that he knew the connection. "We'll have fun today. We're going to the air show!"

"I haven't been to one in years." His father smiled at Addie, but he raised a brow of concern to Jacob. "We can talk later, son. Unless you want to talk now."

And ruin their day? No. He just needed to keep Addie busy and away from the resort. Away from Josie. "Just some work stuff, Dad. No big deal."

Bob Weatherly hadn't raised two kids and run a multistate restaurant chain by being obtuse. "We'll talk anyway. Kid, let's go feed the gulls before we take off, okay?"

"Yes! I love the way they squeal and screech!"

"Are you all right?" His mother wasn't fooled, either. "Jacob, if you need help with something, I'm here. We're here," she corrected herself. "What's wrong?"

He couldn't do this to her. She'd lost enough, and he wasn't about to layer all this grief on her now that she was just getting better. He hadn't seen her this relaxed since Ginger's death, and the last thing he wanted to do was lay more heavy stuff at her door.

He'd handle this himself. He was a smart, educated, successful man. Surely there was some way to defuse this whole mess. Oh, sure, Josie had said she'd back out of the picture, but he had no reason to believe her. Not now, when he realized their budding relationship had been based on a network of lies. "Just end-of-job stuff, Mom. And wanting to make the best possible choices for all concerned."

"Well, your father and I aren't all that enamored with the golden years of retirement. We found that out the hard way," she told him. "You wrap your head around what's best for you and Addie, and we'll make it work. Whatever you two decide is fine with us. We're pretty mobile, your dad and I."

He hugged her. He didn't know how much he needed that hug until he got it, and that only strengthened his resolve. His parents didn't need any more heartbreak on their plate. They'd had more than their share already.

He spent the morning working in his office. He double-checked contractual obligations to the subcontractors and approved nearly a million dollars in final payments. He had his executive assistant produce personalized thank-you notes to every company that had been part of the overall endeavor, a Carrington custom.

And when he got to the name Bayou Barbecue, Josephine Gallagher, owner/manager, anger and disappointment spiked anew.

He wanted to burn the thank-you card. Or crumple it up and throw it away.

Seeing her name reignited his initial concerns of nearly two months before. Why hadn't he paid attention to his gut then? Why had he moved ahead, getting to know her?

Yes, she was beautiful. But he met beautiful women all the time. With Josie, it was something else, something beneath the surface that drew him. To later discover it was all a lie messed with his head.

Was she that good at deceit? Or was he that gullible?

He contacted his job recruiter and told her

to release his interest in the local job, and pursue the Raleigh and Knoxville opportunities, all while wondering if that would be far away enough.

Would she track them down? Would she—

You think she'll stalk you? That's your takeaway? Seriously?

He brewed himself a coffee at the fancy machine Josie had admired, then took it back to his office.

You really think you were falling in love with a traitor? Or maybe there's more to this story?

He knew the truth of the matter. He'd been falling head over heels and she'd lied her way into his affections. Into Addie's affections. He wasn't interested in lame excuses. Maybe he should hire his own lawyer, find out how Josie recognized Addie. Because in a closed adoption, she shouldn't have known anything but the basics. Of course these days, the basics were embellished by a few keystrokes in a Google search, but that required at least a name to search, and he needed to know how she'd acquired that.

He put in a full day.

When the scent of savory meat wafted through the lobby, he ignored it.

When he spotted folks in the sand with Bayou Barbecue paper products, he tried not to think of the woman working behind the scenes. She wasn't who or what he thought she was, and that meant it was all an act.

He avoided talking to his father that night. The reprieve would be short-lived, but he wanted his lawyer to get him the lowdown on the situation, and then hated that it had come to this, with an innocent child trapped in between.

"This is not your fault," the lawyer assured him. "You did nothing wrong, and my job is to get to the bottom of the situation and make sure Addie's place with you is untouchable. You didn't create this debacle. She did. In a game of chess, she made moves to trap your queen. Our only choice now is to countermeasure."

Their only choice?

His conscience niggled him after an hour-long phone call with a pricey attorney, because he'd been in the business side of legal briefs and attorneys and counteroffers long enough. When the lawyers got brought into it, everything took longer.

You could try talking to Josie. You've always taken the direct route, that's why you're good at your job. You reduce the layers of bureaucracy to one-on-one factors.

On buildings, yes. Multimillion-dollar projects needed occasional finessing. He was good at that.

But his child was different. He was different. His pledge to her meant everything.

This time he needed to step back and let someone else do the negotiating, because his head wasn't clear, and if he was truthful with himself?

His heart was muddled, too.

"You warned me, Cruz." Josie brought a wad of tissues to her face on Wednesday night. "You encouraged me to tell him, and I waited too long. And then he wasn't interested in explanations or excuses. He threw the words *wild child* in my face and ordered me to stay away."

Cissy snugged an arm around Josie's shoulders.

Kimberly and Drew were there, and Cruz had left Rory with the kids to touch base on things. "He's hired a lawyer," Cruz told her.

Of course he would. She'd recognized the fear in his face, behind the ice-cold anger. "Understandable. He thinks I'm going for custody."

"Does he even have a clue what brought all this about?" Cissy demanded.

Josie put her hand over her mother's. "Easy, mama bear." When Cissy flushed, Josie hugged her. "It's better this way. Really. We'll let things wind down, they'll leave and life goes on." Her mouth said the words while her heart hung heavy in her chest. "It will get better, Mom. I promise."

"Because you've done this twice before." Kimberly whispered the words, and her face… Kimberly's beautiful face was etched with sorrow. "Josie, I wish I could do something. Anything. I hate that I can't."

"I know." Josie stood and swiped her hands to the sides of her shorts. "We'll keep busy. We'll pray. We'll move on, because the only thing I ever wanted in this whole mess was for my daughter to be happy. And she is. End of story." She dabbed the tissues to her cheeks one last time. "Cruz, call off his lawyer as best you can. I'm keeping a low profile, out of sight, out of mind, and heaven knows I'm busy enough at the restaurant to keep my days full. In time, this too shall pass."

She didn't wait to see if she'd convinced them.

She couldn't.

She'd cry again, and that had been her modus operandi whenever she wasn't at work, so she'd worked long, hard hours for three days straight.

If thoughts of Addie and Jacob swept over her at work, she used an old trick of breathing deep, through her nose. Exhaling slowly, through her mouth. Methods she'd used in the past, that worked still. Picturing silly things, funny things.

But mostly she worked because if her hands were busy, her mind couldn't easily go to the amazing joy that had just been wrenched away from her once again.

Two days left.

Jacob would be finished with his stake in the Eastern Shore project on Friday, and the day couldn't come fast enough. He'd take his four weeks of vacation, and he'd relocate his life away from verdant hills, vineyards, cattle farms, amazing sunrises and prettier sunsets.

Away from here. Away from her.

His assistant buzzed him shortly after two o'clock. "Jacob, there's a Cruz Maldonado to see you. He says he's an attorney."

An unannounced attorney visit could come from only one source: Josie.

He wanted to refuse this guy entrance. He almost barked for him to make an appointment, but Jacob understood the positive effects of just stopping by, utilizing the surprise factor. He'd done that to Josie, that first day. He swallowed what he wanted to say and stayed professional. "Send him in."

He stood, but he wasn't about to reach out

and shake this guy's hand. He kept his expression bland and pretended his blood wasn't boiling inside. "Generally people make appointments to see me, Mr. Maldonado."

"Cruz, please. And frankly, the only reason I'm being this cordial and polite is because you have no idea what's led up to our current state of affairs, and I'm about to fill you in." The other man stood tall, square-shouldered and resolute, as if Jacob was the one causing a problem. The base of his neck went tight. So did his hands.

"Mr. Weatherly, I don't know you," Cruz began.

"Then we're even."

Cruz conceded that with a calm look. "Two months ago, my wife's cousin came to me."

"Josie."

"Yes. And she told me a story that few knew. Certainly no one here was aware of the fact that she had a daughter, or that she'd given up that child for adoption over six years before."

"Once a liar, always a liar?"

Cruz winced and Jacob felt instantly ashamed because he wasn't normally a jerk, but there was nothing normal about the current situation.

"I understand where you're coming from, but that's not how it was. And I'm not here to give you the details. That's up to Josie, if you're man enough to hear them. And that part's up to you." Cruz kept his gaze and tone level. "But let me just say that at no time in all of this was Josie at fault. She endured an unspeakable act, but she found the strength to move forward, put her life on hold in New Orleans to give birth to a child, and researched agencies who would give her child the best possible chance at a strong, balanced family—the kind of family Josie had known, growing up here."

An unspeakable act?

A block of air pushed hard against Jacob's chest, real hard.

"Josie didn't hire a New York lawyer. I did," Cruz continued. "And not to bring havoc on you, but to see what went wrong six years ago."

"Except in a closed adoption, the names are not exchanged." Jacob leaned forward and tightened his expression. "Josie not only knew my sister's name, she recognized Addie when she saw her. Which means she must have been secretly spying on her as she grew up."

Cruz held his gaze for a long moment, long enough for more of that air to tighten Jacob's chest. "Or it could mean that Josie gave up a lobe of her liver to save her daughter's life over three years ago. But your story is good, too."

"She did what?" Jacob pressed his hands

against the flat of his desk. "She was the donor for Addie's surgery?"

"She was. Josie fully respected the contractual agreement of the adoption, but they inserted a clause that in the case of a medical emergency, Josie could be contacted. When Addie got sick, Ginger contacted Sweet Hope. In turn, they called Josie and passed along the information, wondering if she would be tested as a donor. She was a blood match and willingly went ahead with a life-threatening operation because nothing was more important than saving Addie's life. Even though it meant risking hers."

Josie, donating a part of her liver to save Addie's life. Josie, keeping her end of the agreement until she was needed. "You're sure about this?"

"Do you need to see the scar? Or would hospital records at Children's Hospital of Atlanta and Emory do?"

At the moment, Jacob's head felt like it was spinning in circles. "Ginger said—"

"Mr. Weatherly, the further we've gotten into this case, the less anyone should believe things your sister presented as fact." Cruz stayed matter-of-fact but firm as he ticked off his fingers. "She lied to the agency, complicit with her then-husband, then lied to Josie in the hospital by saying Adam was too emotional to come see her, but extended his thanks through a forged note to maintain the charade of a solid marriage."

Lies… Ginger hadn't just stretched the truth, she'd lied as a means to achieve her ends, whatever they were.

"Why would the hospital use a drug user's liver? That can't be right."

Cruz stood. He settled a look on Jacob that questioned more than his words, that maybe questioned him. "Who gave you that information, Mr. Weatherly?"

Now it wasn't just air making his chest tight. It was realization, followed by guilt. "My sister."

"And there you go." Cruz studied him, turned toward the door, then swung back. "Talk to Josie. If you have an ounce of human decency in you, you should go and talk to her face-to-face. Yes, she recognized Addie that first day. She saw her carefully constructed plans to ensure her baby's future had been altered. Her daughter walked onto the property calling a strange man 'Daddy.' So yes, she took steps to find out what happened to the adoptive parents, and then to make sure you weren't a horrible person. Under the circumstances, I think any parent would do the same thing. And just so you know—" he stared at Jacob, long and hard "—if she gives you a chance to talk to her, to hear her story, then consider yourself a fortunate man. Any guy who throws teen-age indiscretions into someone's face is best avoided in my book. But then, Josie might be kinder than I am."

He left.

Jacob stared at the door. He lifted the phone, but who was there to call? The agency?

They'd give their spin on their stated position. He'd already heard that.

His heart wasn't just heavy in his chest. It thrummed like a bass drum, and he probably deserved the headache that came along with it.

Ginger.

Her selfishness had gone too far this time. She'd deceived professionals, his parents, him, even Addie...and of course, the sacrificial mother, giving up the most precious thing in the world, her child. Ginger and Adam had willingly misled the agency as a means to an end—Ginger's wish to be a mother.

Shame knifed him.

He got out of his chair and moved to the window overlooking the southwest corner of the wide, sandy beach. Across the lake treed lots and tapering hills gave way to agricultural spots above. Thick stands of green covered the farthest hills, and the movement of boats, personal watercraft and sailboats dotted the long, slim finger of Canandaigua Lake.

She hadn't come looking for Addie. He and Addie had stumbled onto Josie because of his job, nothing more sinister than that.

His parents needed to know the truth.

He hated that reality. But to keep it from them would be wrong, especially now that others knew what Ginger had done.

And Josie...

He pinched the bridge of his nose, because he owed her an apology. Maybe she'd talk to him. Maybe she wouldn't. That would be her choice. But he couldn't leave without apologizing, because if this woman hadn't been willing to save Addie's life twice, then he'd have no daughter. A gentleman owned his blame and his shame, and in this case, Jacob claimed both. But first, he'd face his parents.

Chapter Fourteen

Friday would be Jacob's last day at the inn. Josie had seen the internal memo thanking him for his service and wishing him well in future endeavors.

He'd be gone. And Addie would be gone.

She couldn't think about it, but she couldn't stop thinking about it, either, wishing she could have one more moment. One more glimpse. But she'd made a promise, and if there was one thing Josie had learned to do, it was to keep her promises.

Terry stepped in to take over at four on Thursday. Josie shed her sauce-splattered work apron and ducked out the back. She ran straight into Jacob's parents and Addie, coming toward her as they aimed for the beach. "Young lady, I was hoping to run into you again!" Bob Weatherly moved her way, smiling.

Josie had nowhere to go, nowhere to hide. She'd promised Jacob she'd stay away from Addie, but she drank in the sight of her as Sheila and Addie approached. "You guys must have had a fun day."

"Amazing!" Addie laughed, and then she did it. She surged forward and grabbed Josie around the middle and wouldn't let go, a hug Josie wished could go on forever. "Oh, Josie, it was so much fun! We went down to the fish hatchy place where they have so many teeny, tiny little fishies and they're all just babies! And then they take them and they let them go in the—" Her forehead knit as she searched for the word.

"Creek," Josie supplied.

"Yes, you know this stuff!" Addie had loosened her grip, but then hugged her again, the best present ever. "So they let them go into the creek and they all go—" She let go of Josie and frowned at Bob. "Where do they go, Pawpaw?"

"The lake. And they grow up in the lake and when they want to have baby fish, they swim back up the very same stream they came from."

"No way! Really?" Josie couldn't help it. She feigned surprise as she lifted a brow. "They know which one to go to?"

"Yes! This is the coolest part! They go to

that very stream and swim up and then the fish hatchy place knows they're doing a good job."

Sheila put a hand on her shoulder. "Hatchery," she corrected in a soft, Southern drawl. And Addie beamed up at her and recreated the word with all the Yankee twang she'd been using for months. "Hatchery."

Sheila sighed, but smiled, too.

"A fine summation," Bob told her, laughing. "So Josie, I was looking around this area, and it seems there have been a bunch of barbecue places scattered around, but not much longevity in them. Why is that?"

"You know the truth in this business better than anyone," she replied. "It's hard to get a restaurant up and running and make enough money to keep it running unless you've got really low overhead. And that's how I started out, with a no-rent, I'll-fix-it-up sweat equity deal. Start-up costs can be a crusher."

"And yet you thrived when others failed."

She started to protest, but she didn't dare carry this chance meeting longer. She made a promise to Jacob, and she didn't want to break it. "Good timing, perhaps."

"Good food," he shot back. "Listen, I'd—"

Her cell phone indicated an incoming text, and she used that as an excuse to break away. She'd made a pledge to leave Addie alone.

Jacob already mistrusted her. She'd gotten her wish of seeing Addie one last time. And that would have to do. She lifted the phone. "I have to tend to this, I'm so sorry."

"Don't be. Just be proud of what you've done here," Bob told her. "It's commendable."

Jacob hadn't told them. If they knew they wouldn't be treating her like this. Would he tell them eventually?

Perhaps, once they were all safe and sound down south. She pulled out her phone, saw the picture Kimberly had sent of baby Elizabeth and sent a smiling emoji in return.

She'd wanted what Kimberly now had. A loving husband, a home and a family. For a little while, the thought of doing that with Jacob and Addie had put her pulse into high gear, but now reality lay at her doorstep. In two days they'd be gone, out of her life.

But not out of her heart.

She was experienced enough to know that wouldn't happen. But with faith and family, she'd ride out this newest wave of sadness. She sent back the picture message to Kimberly with one single word: Amazing, knowing her cousin would understand. She drove back to town, parked alongside the carriage house drive and took a walk. She didn't look at Stan's, remembering Addie's love for frozen custard. And she didn't hit the beach where the local kids loved to gather, splash and play.

She walked by the arching stone walls of Grace Haven Community and saw the door standing open. Sweet voices melded with dancing notes from the keyboardist, drifting up the wide stairway leading to the basement-level classrooms. Thursday night choir practice was in full swing.

She took a place on a pew in the still of the summer's evening. The bank of votives flickered to her right, and to her left, stained glass windows depicted teachings from the New Testament. Children, gathering around Jesus. A shepherd, seeking a lost lamb. A father, embracing two sons. And then one of the condemned woman, in the sand at Jesus's feet. One hand stretched toward her, and the other indicated the empty street around them.

Her accusers had gone, every single one. And there she was, with Christ, an audience of one, needing only God's forgiveness.

Outside, sweet sounds of summer collided in the night. Laughter, shouts and the subtle swish of bike tires on old, village sidewalks.

She'd seen Addie one last time. She'd gotten two final hugs, and that in itself was a treasure. Most important, she knew her child, her most precious gift from God, was in good hands.

All she'd ever wanted was Addie safe and sound and happy. Her wish had been granted, although not by ordinary means.

She tried not to think of Jacob. His gentle eyes, his honest smile, the touch of his hand, the grasp of his fingers, his kiss…

She blinked back emotion and stood.

She'd wished for a chance to say goodbye to Addie. To see her one final time. To realize how perfectly content she was.

That wish had been granted today. Asking for anything more would be just plain greedy, but if she had her way?

She sighed and slipped her purse strap up over her shoulder.

She'd be greedy enough to want it all.

Jacob gestured for his parents to follow him outside. Addie was curled up in the air-conditioned living room of the cottage, watching a favorite show. His mother slid the screen door shut and followed the men to the shaded gazebo overlooking the water. "I've got something to tell you."

"You look serious. Should we sit?"

He grimaced. "Probably wouldn't be a bad idea." They sat and he did, too, trying to figure out the best way to approaching this. In the end, he just told them, straight out. "It's about Ginger, and you're not going to like it."

His father's jaw tightened, but he looked more sad than surprised. He reached out and took his wife's right hand in his left one. "Go on."

"She committed fraud to adopt Addie."

"Tell me you're joking." His father sat more upright. Whatever he was expecting, it certainly wasn't the truth Jacob just laid out for them.

"Jacob. How do you know this?" Quick tears filled his mother's eyes, but she blinked them back and clung to her husband's hand.

Jacob told them the story, detail by detail. The web of lies, the deceit, the double cross of the agency and the birth mother. The *mother*, he corrected himself. And when he was done, his parents weren't as shocked as he thought they'd be. Disappointed, yes. But not blown away by Ginger's illicit choices.

"How did this all come up, son? What made you go digging?"

And now the hard part. But not so hard, either, when he considered Josie's heroic actions to save Addie's life. "Her birth mother lives here. She saw Addie with me and recognized her because Ginger had shown her a picture of Addie at age three, when Addie had the liver transplant. Actually, Addie's biological mother was the living donor for Addie's transplant."

"She was?" Now Sheila put a hand to her chest. "But Ginger said—"

"I know. She told us that Addie's mother was a drug user and that Addie's liver came from someone on the transplant match list who requested anonymity. That part was true, because Addie's mother didn't want to mess up Addie's life. But she was no drug user. She'd experimented with a few things in college, years before, but Ginger made it seem like she'd deliberately saved Addie from life with an addict."

"Yes, she did. Why, I wonder?"

"Because it made her feel nobler?" Jacob had spent a lot of time trying to reason this out, too. "Or less guilty for bilking you guys out of that thirty thousand she claimed was for the birth mother? Because the file firmly states that the mother refused any payment for her role in carrying the child, and that all medical costs were paid for by the mother's insurance and her own funds. When Addie's mother came to Atlanta to save Addie's life, Ginger pretended that she and Adam were still together. She claimed Adam was too overcome with worry about Addie to do anything more than send a note. And here it is." He handed them the forged note. "For some reason the agency had a copy in the file. They faxed it to me."

"Not Adam's handwriting," his mother pointed out.

"And almost three years after he'd left the family."

"Wait." His father looked at the note more closely, then swallowed hard. "This note is thanking Josie…" He studied Jacob. "Is Josie Gallagher Addie's real mother?"

"Yes."

"Oh, that poor woman." Sheila grabbed hold of Jacob's arm. "She's had her daughter here all this time, under her nose, and couldn't acknowledge her?"

Jacob hadn't thought he could feel worse. "Yes."

"And her mother must know. The resemblance between Cissy and Addie is so clear now. Jacob, what are we going to do? How can we fix this?"

A question he'd been asking himself for hours now. "I don't know. I'm going to go see her, but I need Addie to stay here overnight. If that's all right."

"It's more than all right, it's fine, I just…" Sheila wrung her hands, but she didn't fall apart. If anything, this information seemed to make her stronger. "Jacob, if there's anything we can do, just let us know." She frowned, distraught. "I wasn't overtly aware that Ginger was up to anything during the adoption proceedings, but I sensed it. And yet, I so desperately wanted her happy. She wasn't like you, son." She reached out and hugged him as she had the other night. "She was never happy and never satisfied, always wanting more. But I never imagined she'd go so far as to lie about something as important and special as an adoption."

"Are you going to see Josie tonight?" his father asked.

He had little choice. She'd be busy all day tomorrow and Saturday, the crazy, pumped-up hours of running a beachside restaurant midsummer. "Yes. And I wouldn't mind a few prayers coming my way."

His father clapped a hand onto his shoulder, firm and strong. "I think we can manage that."

"And please, Jacob, please…" His mother grasped his two hands in hers. "Tell her how very sorry we are for all of her pain. My heart truly goes out to her."

His mother hadn't jumped to conclusions as he had. His father was willing to pray for him to find some way to make peace with Josie, and he couldn't remember the last time Bob Weatherly prayed and meant it.

He kissed Addie good-night and hurried to his car.

Would she be at the carriage house apartment? Or with family? Should he message her or just show up?

He didn't want to give her the chance to reject his visit before he got there, so surprise won. He drove into the village, parked on the street and walked up the Gallagher driveway. Evening sun brightened the twin dormered windows facing the drive over the three-car garage. He stared up at them, then strode forward, determined, but then ground to a complete stop when a voice—her voice—came from behind.

"What are you doing here, Jacob?"

He turned.

She stood straight and tall, facing him. She kept her arms at her sides, and the loose, lacy top flowed over her hips while the sleeves did the same thing over her slim, tanned hands.

"I need to talk to you."

She didn't move closer. She didn't look angry. She looked bereft. And that made his heart ache harder. "You've had your say. Please go."

He couldn't, so he shook his head. "It's not that easy."

"Easy?" Her gold-green eyes flashed fire his way. "Trust me, there is not one moment of this entire thing that could possibly be construed as easy, Jacob. Not from where I'm standing."

"Can we talk? Please?" He needed to talk to her. Explain what he knew. And perhaps more important, he needed to listen for a change, and not assume he had all the answers. "Can we walk down by the water?"

"It's too busy there, and I don't need the entire town talking about me again. I've had my share of that, thank you."

"Josie, I—"

"This way." Abrupt, she led him through the garage and up the stairs. Cool air greeted them when she opened the upper door, and she led the way through a galley kitchen, into a cozy living room beyond. She held up her watch. "You've got ten minutes."

"Josie."

"Clock's ticking."

He sat, hoping she'd sit, too, and when he swiped his damp hands against his trousers, she noticed, but it wasn't sympathy that deepened her gaze. She sat on the love seat opposite him, unhappy and untrusting. His fault, he knew. "Cruz Maldonado came to see me."

She breathed deeply and said nothing, but she brought her hands together in her lap and held them there.

"He explained what he'd found. What the

agency revealed, and how my sister lied to get what she wanted, which turned out to be your daughter." He paused, then shook his head. "I don't get it, Josie. What my sister did. It's incomprehensible to me. We were raised by the same parents, but I could never do what she did. I don't lie. I don't take advantage. Ginger did, every chance she got, but I don't think any of us ever expected it to go to this level. To lie and then further confirm that lie to gain what she wanted. To deceive a mother." He leaned forward and wished she'd look at him, but she kept her eyes down. "I'm sorry, Josie. So very sorry. My parents feel the same way. Shocked and ashamed."

"They know?"

Now her eyes came to his.

He nodded. "I had to tell them. If we're going to work this thing out, they need to know everything."

"There's nothing to work out." Calm and steadfast, she held his attention. "You're leaving. Addie is wonderfully happy with you, and that's all I ever wanted, Jacob. I didn't go into the adoption agency with thoughts of control. I just wanted the decisions I made, the requirements I wanted for her, to be respected."

"And they weren't."

"No. But one thing I've learned from this

whole thing is to stop looking back. I made mistakes, sure. I did stupid things in college and paid the price by shaming my mother and my brothers. But that's behind me now. God forgave me. And after a long time and a lot of self-shaming, I learned to forgive myself." She glanced at her watch, implying his time was nearly up. "Addie's in good hands. No, wait." She drew a breath and indicated him with a wave. "She's in great hands. I could never mess that up. What kind of selfish person wrenches a child away from someone who loves her unconditionally?" She shrugged. "Not me."

"And Addie's father wanted nothing to do with her?" He laid the words out gently, watching. Would she talk to him? Share her story? Or block him out? He wouldn't blame her if she did, not after he'd ranted and raved.

She didn't look up this time. Eyes down, he saw a tear slip and fall, onto her hand. And then another.

Help her, Lord. Help her to see I'm not the enemy. That I seek her forgiveness and understanding and maybe more... Help her to trust me. Please.

"You should go." Soft words in a small voice.

He got up, but he didn't go. He changed seats and sat down beside her, close enough to feel her breath, but not touching. "What happened,

Josie?" That, just that, an invitation to trust. Would she take it?

She shouldn't after what he'd said and done, but he wanted her to. He longed for her to. She breathed softly, then lifted one pretty, tanned shoulder. "I trusted the wrong man, Jacob. After years of being so careful and prim and proper in a city where that's not exactly easy, I believed a man who carried date-rape drugs in his pocket. A foolish mistake from a woman who had promised her family nothing would go wrong in New Orleans. And there I was, hating myself all over again, but pregnant this time. All I wanted, Jacob—" she turned and faced him now, twin tear tracks running down her pretty cheeks "—was for my child to have the best possible start I could give her. A loving family, parents who cherished her and a normal future. So when I signed those papers in good faith, I expected the same in return. To discover it was all built on lies made me angry. So angry. Not at you."

She paused, looking away, gathering her thoughts. "But at the callousness of going after a child by lying. Waving money around. Deceiving me. Addie's conception was caused by deceit. I couldn't bear to think that her life revolved around that, too. And so I had you checked out."

His heart twisted in pain, hearing her words, imagining being alone, betrayed and a single mother.

"I promised myself I'd never let that happen again."

"Josie, I—"

She stood and crossed through the kitchen to the door. "Time's up, Jacob. It's time for both of us to move on to the lives God has laid out for us. My concerns have been put to rest, and I wish you nothing but goodness, all of your days." She pulled the door open. "Goodbye."

She left him no choice. He wasn't there to browbeat her, but to empathize. He'd done that and now... He paused at the door, willing her to look up. Just once.

She didn't. Chin down, she made no eye contact. He longed to tip that chin up. To promise her things would be okay. Could be okay.

But a tiny thought niggled within, a reminder that actions spoke louder than words. He touched her shoulder softly, gently. "God bless you, Josie."

He left, and when the soft click of the door separated them, he trudged to his car.

So much hurt. So much heartbreak. A ridiculous amount, in fact. To have two people, bound by love of a child, caring for one another, and driven apart by anger.

A glimmer of his dream returned, but he'd thrown mean, harsh words at an innocent woman. Why would she want to care? And would winning her for Addie's sake be enough?

He knew it wouldn't. He wanted Josie Gallagher's love for *his* sake. The amazingly wonderful kid was pure bonus.

He went home to the empty apartment, sat down and didn't dwell.

He acted.

He opened his laptop to scout out real estate opportunities. He messaged his recruiter about the local job he'd passed on.

She messaged back quickly that it was gone, but she'd check for other possibilities.

Never mind, he decided as he messaged a local Realtor. There were other jobs. Maybe not perfect, but he realized now how he'd nearly turned his back on practically perfect, and it had nothing to do with work and everything to do with faith, hope and love. *And the greatest of these was love.*

That paraphrased line from Corinthians became his new mantra.

He made a list of properties for sale in Grace Haven, and remembered to check their proximity to cows or the amount of acreage needed to have a cow. He had no idea how to take care of a cow, but he could learn. If it gave him the chance to win Josie's heart, he could learn just about anything.

And if she didn't fall in love with him? He didn't want to imagine that outcome, but at least she wouldn't be denied access to her child. The very idea was unthinkable. They'd have to talk things through, but to leave Grace Haven and separate mother and child was wrong, and Jacob Weatherly had always made a point of not doing wrong. He intended to keep that trend going.

He got up in the morning, showered and shaved, ready for his last day of work with Carrington. He'd had a solid history with them, but the time had come to lay down roots. Roots strong enough to help Addie grow wings. That was his goal now. To lay down roots in Grace Haven, New York.

Chapter Fifteen

Josie put Terry on smoker detail early Friday, and monitored his progress as the day went on.

She didn't give one thought to Jacob's gentle gaze. His kind words. His obvious sympathy for what had taken place long ago.

And she absolutely, positively refused to think about his scent when he took a seat next to her, the smell of fading aftershave, minty breath and fresh lake breezes.

And she would not contemplate his touch, that gentle stroke of his big, strong hand to her shoulder, putting her in mind of that heart-stopping kiss shared not long ago.

She refused to think about any of it, but she couldn't seem to think of anything else. She thought of him as she steamed basmati rice. She pictured him as they filled the big barbecue drum with Cajun-blackened split chickens, a Friday special. And when the fish and seafood order came in, she thought about Lake Ontario, and their beautiful day of sun and sand.

She thought of him as they warmed peppered cheese for nachos.

And she couldn't help but think about him as she watched the sous chef mix a monster-size vat of coleslaw while she tossed together her own version of hot potato salad alongside. Nothing was a big enough distraction.

He shouldn't have come.

He could have left town quietly, as planned, but no. He showed up, being kind and good and understanding.

He was kind and good and understanding last night. Last week? Not so much.

She heard the internal warning clearly, and got the gist. He'd turned on her when he thought she'd deceived him for her own purposes.

He could have asked, her conscience prodded when she finally closed the door on the restaurant at nearly ten o'clock that evening.

But a part of Josie was glad he'd leaped to protecting Addie first. That's what a dad did, right? Her father had been like that, and when he'd died, she'd lost that sense of being safe and protected. Maybe that's why she'd been fool-ish in college. Either way, she'd appreciated her father's strong stance on life and love and family. And she felt the same way about Jacob with Addie.

She walked to her car. The sun had gone down minutes before, the elongated days of summer lingering well past nine. Shadows deepened as she walked, and when she got to the car, there was a note taped to the windshield window. "Dear Miss Josie..."

Her heart melted instantly.

"Will you come on a date with me and my dad on Monday?" Addie had crossed out an *f* on the word *wif* and corrected it with a *th*, indicating someone helped the six-year-old pen the letter in bright red crayon on faded construction paper.

Why was he doing this? She'd cut things off deliberately. Was he feeling some sense of misguided guilt? Or...

And she didn't even begin to dare hope this.

Was he still interested?

You think?

The voice in her head sounded a little sarcastic. She tucked the note into her purse, shushed the voice and climbed into the car.

She found another note waiting for her at the garage door, on blue paper this time.

"Meet us in your driveway at ten o'clock. Please. XXX OOO."

And then on the bottom she'd added: "On Monday."

She should text Jacob and tell him no. Wasn't it foolish to hang out with Addie, only to lose her all over again? And yet, when would she get another chance?

Perhaps never.

At the top of the stairs she found a third note. "Text YES to 404-555-4101."

He'd covered the bases. With Addie.

She walked inside the apartment. Cool air met her, and after working in a hot, sweat-inducing kitchen on a hot summer's day, the air felt good. So good.

She cleaned up and eyed the third note, then picked up her phone and texted one quick word. Yes.

She put down the phone, half-afraid he wouldn't text back, and just as afraid he would. And when he did, she lifted the phone quickly to see what he said.

We're so glad.

Just that.

Her heart jittered. So did her breath. She wouldn't read too much into this, because there were two days to wait, but seeing those notes and that text soothed her heart and her soul. Josie Gallagher got her first good night's sleep since seeing Addie hop out of that car nearly two months before.

"Mom. Dad. Addie and I have something to tell you." Jacob snugged his arm around Addie's shoulders and faced his parents on Saturday morning. "We're going to stay in Grace Haven."

"Like forever," Addie added helpfully when his parents didn't react.

"I'm looking at houses…"

"And cows," chimed in Addie. "But we're not really exactly sure what color cow to get, so I think Farmer Gallagher can help us decide. Maybe."

He watched his parents exchange a look, then his father rose, crossed the floor and handed him a sheaf of papers. "See what you think."

What he thought? Jacob examined the top copy, then leafed through the sheets below before shifting his attention back to his father. "You want to franchise the Bayou Barbecue?"

"If Josie will let me, yes."

"Dad, I—" He clutched the paperwork, dumbfounded.

"It's an amazing opportunity," his father went on. "There's nothing up here that holds a candle to her cooking, and I saw that right off. If we open several different spots, dotting the county, at least this one and the next one, we've got the entire Rochester market covered, and it's a perfect time to jump into New York business. They're doing tax incentives like crazy for the next decade. No time like the present, Jacob, and I am sick to death of retirement. Are you interested?"

"Interested?"

His father pointed to the papers. "In running the show? I'll be here to launch with you, but I have no intention of staying up north all year, every year. A man would have to be daft to think such a thing, and Mother and I would still have a few months of calm and quiet along the Gulf Coast. And then I would come back and jump in. It's in your wheelhouse, son. It's what you do best. Build things and oversee restaurant quality."

Addie squealed once she realized what the exchange meant. "Dad, let's do it! Oh, won't Josie be pleased!"

"Will she?" He aimed a look of question at his father.

Bob shrugged. "We won't know until we ask her, so I invited her over tomorrow after her shift. She's done early, so mother's planning a four o'clock supper in the gazebo. She wanted to have it catered, but I think Josie's more the hots and hamburgers type."

"She said yes?"

"Well, I did my fair share of sweet-talking, so in the end, there was little else to say."

Addie grabbed hold of Jacob's arm. "That means I don't have to wait until Monday to see my mom!"

Sheila's eyes went wide when Addie slapped a hand over her mouth.

Jacob nodded. "I'm not big on secrets, and I explained that Josie loved her so much that she wanted to find a nice home, the nicest home ever for Addie to be in. But when unexpected things happened, God brought her and me here, right here, to Grace Haven. We didn't know her mother lived here. But God did. And now we do, too. Now all that's left is for us to find a place."

"I'm going to surprise Josie and tell her when I see her, so we have to keep it a big secret. Okay?" Addie grabbed his parents' hands, imploring.

"It's very okay." Bob scooped her up and gave her a big hug. Sheila joined him, her arms wrapped around him and the girl. And when Addie dashed off to make pictures of how she perceived her new life, including a full menagerie of animals, he turned to his parents. "I hope it's all right that I told her. I didn't mean to spring it on you guys like that."

"Better the truth than a lie, Jacob. Always." His mother looked sad but resolute. "It's our turn to fix things, and I'm not afraid to do my share."

"Me, either," declared Bob. "If I'm going to have a working relationship with that fine young woman, I want it off on the right foot from the get-go. And now, I'm going to stop by Henderson Architectural and see if they can make my thoughts look a little better than these chicken scratches I did on my own. I want Josie to see this the way I picture it. Might help persuade her to my way of thinking."

"And you and Addie have some errands to run?" Sheila asked.

"We do." Jacob palmed Addie's head and grinned. "We're going to spend the day exploring and seeing if any of the properties Miss Linda wants to show us are just right."

"Then we'll see you tomorrow. And Jacob?"

"Yes?" He turned.

"Your dad and I were wondering which church you go to. Just in case we're up in time and have a mind to go."

"We like lots of them, but I like Grace Haven Community best, Memaw." Sincerity marked Addie's earnest look. "It's got the best candles."

"And there you go." Jacob flashed his mother

a smile. "The candles take it, every time. Service begins at nine."

"Nine?" She didn't sound delighted about the early hour, but she didn't wince, either. "Nine it is."

Chapter Sixteen

Dinner with Jacob's parents?

Josie left the Bayou in Terry's capable hands a little after two on Sunday, wishing she hadn't let Bob Weatherly talk her into coming over.

She went home, showered and slipped into a soft, flowy shirt and midlength thin cotton skirt, the kind that swirled with each breath of wind.

She blew-dry her hair and brought it over her shoulder in a long, simple braid, then fastened hoop earrings to her ears, before finishing the look with a long, beachy shell necklace.

A business deal…

That's what Bob Weatherly had said when he stopped by the barbecue kitchen on Saturday morning. He didn't mention Addie, or Jacob, or their unusually convoluted attachment. He simply smiled, complimented her on the food again and asked her to supper.

She'd faced him, squashed her nerves and accepted graciously.

And now she figured she was about to get sick to her stomach with a war of nerves.

She turned onto Sunrise Road, almost directly across the lake from the Eastern Shore Inn.

The road entrance was flanked by woods, but as the road approached the water, the view flared before her. Pretty homes, waterfront tones, shady trees and an amazing view.

She'd grown up in the village, close enough to the beach to be a water baby, but in a much more humble setting than the western shore of Canandaigua Lake.

Their driveway sloped to her left. She parked the car in the shade of wide-trunked maples and slipped out of the seat.

Cool shade softened the thick July air. And a whispered breeze made the leaves dance above, shifting a shimmering pattern of light.

"Beautiful."

Jacob's voice, from a few feet away. She deliberately pretended to misunderstand and turned while motioning to the trees, the house, the setting. "It is."

He smiled.

He didn't correct her, or tease, he simply smiled, knowing she'd get it. And she did. "Do you know what this is about and should I be forewarned?"

He fell into step beside her. "Only if you're the sort who ruins Christmas by sneaking a peek ahead of time."

"I did that once, and ruined the entire day."

"A lesson learned. Hey, kid."

Addie flew their way in a brightly patterned sundress. "Look! We're both wearing dresses! I really, really think we're so much alike!"

Such sweet words and emotion! Josie sank down to her level. "Except that yours has flowers and my skirt has vines."

"I really like it." Addie tipped her gaze up to Josie and studied her with a look of intensity. "It's so beautiful on you."

"Well, thank you. And I must say that I'm quite partial to yours." Addie grabbed Josie's hand, then Jacob's with her other hand, linking them as they rounded the lakeside home.

The waterside gazebo was laid out for a casual summer supper. Long, flowing sheers draped the openings, offering shade as needed. A table that would easily fit eight was centered inside, surrounded by built-in benches. "What a lovely setting. Mrs. Weatherly, this is gorgeous."

Jacob's mother came forward and clasped Josie's hands. "Josie Gallagher, I want to thank you." She squeezed Josie's hands lightly, quietly accentuating her meaning. "I cannot begin to tell you what your kind and sacrificial heart has meant to our family. Thank you." She reached out and hugged Josie. "For blessing us."

"Now, ladies, this is a business meeting, and I don't recall drama being listed on the menu." Bob Weatherly motioned her toward a side table, set up in the shade of another mature tree. "Business first, or food?"

"If I don't like the business, do I still get the food?"

"Absolutely not." He smiled, teasing.

"Then let's eat." She met Bob Weatherly's smile and matched it.

"Josie, you wouldn't believe how many fun things my dad and I do now that he's not working! It's totally amazing!"

Two days of amazing. That was the sweet innocence of a child.

Jacob brought a plate of fresh burgers and Zweigle's hot dogs to the table. "Mom was thinking formal. The rest of us outvoted her, so it's mac salad, burgers and hot dogs."

"My favorites," Josie assured them. "Except for amazing barbecue, that is."

"Exactly the reason I brought you over," Bob

jumped in, impatient. Clearly waiting until after dinner was too much to ask. "Josie, I've got a proposition for you."

"Dad, I thought you were going to let her eat first?" Jacob pointed to the hot food on the table.

"Food tastes best when we're happy," Bob said. He sat down next to Josie and opened a loose-leaf portfolio. "Here's my plan."

The simple prospectus was outlined on the face page. And the simple offer was enough to capture Josie's attention. "You want to franchise the Bayou Barbecue?"

"That's exactly what I want to do. A partnership. You. Me. Him." He pointed over his shoulder to Jacob, and Josie had to sip water to keep from choking. "You provide the dive design and recipes, I build, Jacob oversees the entire operation. Easy, right?"

Easy if you had millions of dollars to invest. She stared at the paper, then the two men. She didn't want to ask the question with Addie right there, but the coincidence of timing wasn't lost on her. "Mr. Weatherly, you know I'm not looking for anything, don't you, sir? That was never my intent."

"Young lady, I believe I fell in love with your food before anything else occurred, and while I pride myself on being a Southern gentleman, that mode does not inspire me to invest a small fortune into a new business endeavor. Great food, however, which fills a dearth in a market niche, does. This—" he tapped the cover sheet lightly "—is all business. The rest?" He raised a glass of sweet tea as if in her honor. "I'm leaving up to you."

"I need to think on it. Seriously think on it. Read it," she added. "And pray."

"I'm in no rush, but once you give me the green light, it will be full steam ahead. Son, these burgers smell perfect."

Simple delicious food, grilled by Jacob, and salad mixed by Bob's own hands.

A lovely afternoon, calm and peaceful, but awkward, too. She couldn't address her relationship to Addie, and Jacob's parents seemed just as reticent.

Did she spark memories of their lost daughter? Good ones? Bad ones?

By eight o'clock she begged off an evening boat ride. "It has been a long week, and it seems I've got a date in the morning," Josie reminded Addie when she asked her to stay longer. "I'll see you then, okay?"

"Okay." Then Addie won her heart further when she wrapped her arms around Josie's waist and whispered, "I just miss you when you're gone. That's all."

"I miss you, too. How nice that I won't have to miss you for long because I'll see you in fourteen hours. Okay?"

"'Kay."

She waved goodbye as she eased out of the awkward driveway, then waved from the road as Jacob and Addie watched her go.

Bob's offer gave her a lot to consider, and a lot to think over.

If Jacob took the job to oversee this project, did that mean they'd be staying in Grace Haven? And if they did—

Heat climbed her cheeks with this next thought…

Was he interested in her? Was he falling in love with her like she was with him? And could they honestly forget the past? And what about Addie? How could she ever tell Addie the truth?

Chapter Seventeen

She went to bed with more questions than answers, and woke up the same way.

By ten o'clock she was ready, and when Jacob rolled his upscale SUV into the driveway, she climbed into the front seat, high-fived Addie behind her and fastened her seat belt.

"I didn't think you could beat last night's look, but you did." Jacob checked out her lace top and the loose capris, cinched in with a turquoise scarf that matched her earrings. "I feel like I'm picking up a Native American princess, which must come from your father's side because your mother is way too fair."

"My Grandma Gallagher was Cherokee, so my dad was part Native American," she replied. "But he definitely favored the Cherokee side of the family. Me, too."

"Do you look like your daddy, Josie?"

She made a face at Addie. "Well, I think I'm a combination of my Grandma Gallagher and my Grandma Moore. I look like both of them. It's funny how things skip generations sometimes," she went on as Jacob turned into a driveway just a few minutes into their trip. "Is this where we're going? The Soules' house?"

"Yup." Jacob climbed out and Addie followed.

Josie got out at a slower pace. "Do you know them?"

"I don't. But she does." He pointed as one of the successful local Realtors pulled into the driveway behind them. "Linda's going to show us some houses. Did I forget to mention that?"

He'd moved closer, gazing down into her eyes, and his expression teased. "I'm sure I meant to say something, Josie."

"You're staying."

"Yes!" Addie fist-pumped the air and grabbed Josie. "I've been dying to tell you that, but Dad said I have to learn to be good about keeping secrets, the good ones, you know, the kind that surprise people with good stuff?"

Linda had come up alongside them. "Does she stop for air?"

"Not as a rule," Jacob replied.

"Ah, the excitement of youth." Linda motioned toward the classic hillside home. "Let's check this one out first, shall we?"

She moved ahead to unlock the door of the pretty brick split-level overlooking the water.

"There are others to see?"

"Several," Jacob told her as they walked toward the door. "Because sometimes you know you need to keep on shopping, Josie. Other times…" He cradled her cheek with his hand, and his eyes said more. Much more. "…you know you've already got the best thing that could ever happen to you."

"Jacob, I—"

"Let's check it out." He led her forward, and they spent the next two hours house hunting, looking at granite countertops and fancy fireplaces and lofted ceilings. All beautiful, all upscale, and not one of them exactly right.

And then they pulled into a log cabin ranch, tucked into the hills as if it was part of them, and Josie let out a breath. "The clearing there, for a garden. And down below, too. But mostly woods, and how perfect for a play area, Jacob. Right there. And can you imagine it trimmed with colored Christmas lights, shining through the woods at night?"

He could, now that he'd seen it through her eyes. Addie raced around the yard, looking this way and that. "I love this one the most, Dad! It's the most perfect house ever! What do you guys think? Can we get it?"

Josie started to back away from the conversation, but Jacob slipped an arm around her waist and wouldn't let her go. "What do you think? It's not in a neighborhood, and tucked away just enough to offer privacy with a view."

"You remembered."

"I did." He locked his hands around her waist, refusing to let her go. "Do you love it?"

"Well, yes…" The log cabin house was beautiful. Wonderful. But nothing compared to the man holding her, or the child running free between the trees.

"And what about me, Josie?" He leaned closer and feathered the lightest of kisses to her mouth, teasing. Tempting. "Do you think you could love me as much as the house, darling?"

"More." She leaned into the circle of his arm and gazed up at him as Addie came their way again. "So much more."

"You both love it? Does that mean we can buy it, Mom? Dad?"

Mom? Josie's heart beat faster. Her pulse sped up. She turned around, certain Addie had misspoken.

"Do you love it, Mom?" Sea-green eyes gazed up at her. "Do you love us?"

"I told her who you are on Saturday." Jacob kept a light grip on Josie's waist, a gentle hand of support. "I told her she had the bravest, coolest, most beautiful mom in the entire world and that God must have brought us here to Grace Haven so we could find you. And love you. So, Josie." He tugged Addie into the circle of his other arm. "Would you do us the honor of marrying us? Of being Addie's mom and my beautiful wife? And most likely running a crazy-busy business if my father has his way?"

Honor.

She'd felt less than honorable too often in her life. To hear that phrase from Jacob, from the man she loved, a man who now knew everything about her and still loved her...

She bent and hugged her daughter.

Her daughter.

And then lifted Addie right up into her arms and held her close while she stretched up for Jacob's sweet kiss. "Why, yes, Mr. Weatherly, Miss Weatherly," she stated in the most Southern of Southern drawls she could muster. "I would be right pleased to be your wife and her sweet mama. And you might be overseeing that chain of restaurants on your own from time to time, Jacob darling, because I do believe Miss Addie put in a heartfelt request for brothers and sisters like normal folks do. And if we grant her that wish…" He grinned when she stretched up for another kiss, longer this time. "…I'm going to be taking a little time off."

"Not too much, right?" He was teasing her, and she loved it.

"Enough so our babies will always know their mom and dad love them more than anything in this world."

Linda cleared her throat nearby. "Forget somebody?"

"Guilty." Jacob laughed as he turned her way. "But the lady said yes, so we're ready to make an offer, and the sooner the better. My apartment lease is up in six weeks, and it would be good to start our new lives, and the new school year, living here."

"I'll get things rolling right now."

A home. A family. A husband. Her daughter. *Their* daughter, she realized.

Two months ago she'd lost her business, her apartment, and envied her cousin Kimberly's dream life. And now the dream was hers, right here in Grace Haven. As Jacob took her hand to walk into their new home, Addie raced ahead, bright, happy and wholesome. And Josie realized it couldn't possibly get better than it was right now.

Epilogue

"This long, trailing veil makes the look, Josie June." Cissy Gallagher spread the ivory veil over the back of Josie's embroidered satin gown on a sun-soaked mid-October Saturday. "This whole effect is perfect for you." *Sniff. Sniff.*

"You promised you wouldn't cry," Josie pretended to scold, but she couldn't. Not really.

"I know." Cissy squared her shoulders, resolute. "If I'm walking my daughter down the aisle, I need to be stoic and strong."

Kate thrust a handful of tissues into Cissy's hand. "Just in case. And may I remind you that I cried at every one of my girl's weddings. It's a mother's prerogative. Now, do we have something old?"

Josie pointed to a nearby table. "Grandma's handkerchief in my emergency bag."

"And the dress is something new. Something borrowed?"

"Kimberly's long slip because they're ridiculously expensive for one day."

Her frugal choice inspired her mother's smile. "That's my girl."

"And something blue," Aunt Kate finished.

Jacob surprised her by stepping into the bride's room with Addie as Aunt Kate spoke. "That's our cue."

"Jacob." Josie turned, smiling, glad he'd broken protocol. Just seeing him eased the war of nerves racing inside her.

"This is a present from us." He and Addie crossed the bride's room and handed Josie a small package. "We went to the jewelry store and they made us something special."

"Special for all three of us," added Addie, excited.

Josie opened the small box and sighed when she spotted the pendant necklace inside. "Jacob. It's gorgeous."

"It's us!" Addie wriggled with delight when Josie bent low. "The coppery stones are for you, the blue part is for Dad, and the green part is me! It matches our eyes!"

"And twines us all together. Just the way it should be." The interwoven pendant bound all three colors together in an unbreakable bond. "Jacob, will you fasten it for me?"

"Happily."

He slipped the delicate necklace from the box and draped it around her neck while Cissy held the veil aside. His fingers fumbled the clasp at first, but then a tiny *click* indicated success.

He left his hands there for just a moment while Kate held up a hand mirror. "Do you like it?"

"Not like. Love. And I love both of you." She smiled at him through the mirror, then down at Addie. "Thank you, both. I'll cherish this forever."

"The feeling's mutual, darlin'." He kissed her cheek, then Addie's. "Are you ladies about ready to meet me up front? Because it looks like there's a crowd gathering."

"I'm ready," announced Addie.

"Me, too." Kim handed the baby off to her mother in time to take her place as matron of honor.

Josie trailed one finger to the beautiful pendant just below her throat. "I love you, Jacob."

He paused. He didn't joke. He didn't tease. He simply looked at her, then Addie, then her again. "I know, darlin'. I know. And the feeling's mutual."

And when she stepped into the church moments later, her arm tucked through her mother's, Josie didn't see the packed pews, or the smiles, or the cell phones raised for pictures.

She saw Jacob, her beloved, standing at the altar, waiting for her. With her daughter trailing floral petals before her, Josie walked toward her dream come true.

* * * * *

If you loved this story,
pick up the other books
in the GRACE HAVEN *series*
from author Ruth Logan Herne

AN UNEXPECTED GROOM
HER UNEXPECTED FAMILY
THEIR SURPRISE DADDY
THE LAWMAN'S YULETIDE BABY

Available now from Love Inspired!

Find more great reads
at www.LoveInspired.com

Dear Reader,

Life isn't always fair. Sometimes bad things happen to good people, and we could spend a lot of time questioning God's will and arguing why, but in the end we still have choices. To put bad and evil behind us and move on with our lives…or to wallow in anger.

Josie Gallagher doesn't wallow. She took charge of a bad situation, trying to act in the best interests of her daughter, but when she realizes her intentions were thwarted by another's deceit, she has no choice but to check things out. In the end, she stays true to her King Solomon beliefs: A true mother will never pull her child apart.

Jacob Weatherly became a father by default, but he's a good, God-fearing man, determined to tip his daughter's life in happy, normal directions. His fear at losing her is palpable and understandable, and it isn't until Josie and Jacob embrace the sacrificial nature of being a true parent that they realize God's timing.

Have you ever faced cruel decisions, only to find out later things worked out for the best?

God's timing isn't always clear to us…but as long as it's clear to Him, we're okay!

I love to hear from readers! Email me at loganherne@gmail.com or visit my website ruthloganherne.com, friend me on Facebook/Ruth Logan Herne or find me cooking at the Yankee Belle Café (www.yankeebellecafe.blogspot.com) with several other Love Inspired authors who love to share their joy of cooking, baking, God and romance with readers!

Thank you for taking the time to read Josie and Jacob's beautiful story, and may God bless you!

Ruthy

Get 2 Free Books,
Plus 2 Free Gifts—
just for trying the Reader Service!

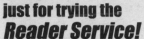

YES! Please send me 2 FREE Love Inspired® Suspense novels and my 2 FREE mystery gifts (gifts are worth about $10 retail). After receiving them, if I don't wish to receive any more books, I can return the shipping statement marked "cancel." If I don't cancel, I will receive 4 brand-new novels every month and be billed just $5.24 each for the regular-print edition or $5.74 each for the larger-print edition in the U.S., or $5.74 each for the regular-print edition or $6.24 each for the larger-print edition in Canada. That's a savings of at least 13% off the cover price. It's quite a bargain! Shipping and handling is just 50¢ per book in the U.S. and 75¢ per book in Canada*. I understand that accepting the 2 free books and gifts places me under no obligation to buy anything. I can always return a shipment and cancel at any time. The free books and gifts are mine to keep no matter what I decide.

Please check one: ☐ Love Inspired Suspense Regular-Print   ☐ Love Inspired Suspense Larger-Print
(153/353 IDN GMWT)   (107/307 IDN GMWT)

Name _____ (PLEASE PRINT) _____

Address _____ Apt. # _____

City _____ State/Prov. _____ Zip/Postal Code _____

Signature (if under 18, a parent or guardian must sign) _____

Mail to the **Reader Service:**
IN U.S.A.: P.O. Box 1341, Buffalo, NY 14240-8531
IN CANADA: P.O. Box 603, Fort Erie, Ontario L2A 5X3

Want to try two free books from another line?
Call 1-800-873-8635 or visit www.ReaderService.com.

Get 2 Free Books,
Plus 2 Free Gifts—
just for trying the
Reader Service!

HOME on the RANCH